THE TRAP?

Katherine started to rap on the door, when she heard Janet's voice, and realized that the other woman was on the phone. She hesitated, as Janet said, "I'm trying to get her to stay on indefinitely."

Katherine drew back, realizing that Janet was talking about her.

"Now don't act like a spoiled child," she continued. "Her coming here has started me thinking . . . about *everything*." There was a little silence, and then, "A danger? What makes you think that?"

This time there was a much longer silence, and when Janet spoke again, her voice was clear and hard. "Yes, she could upset the applecart, start probing. Does that frighten you, Howard?"

A burst of sound from below drowned out her next words, but Katherine was aware that there had been a subtle change in Janet's attitude—a change that spelled danger to her!

Beyond Recall

Dorothy Fletcher

PRESTIGE BOOKS • NEW YORK

BEYOND RECALL

PRESTIGE BOOKS INC. • 18 EAST 41ST STREET
NEW YORK, N.Y. 10017

Chapter 1

When I first heard from Janet Lance after all those years it was like being plunged back into childhood; it was like a return to the past. Since I had last seen Janet she had left the East Coast for the West, had eventually married, borne children and the yearly exchange of Christmas cards had stopped long ago.

I, on my part, had completed art school in New York City, had done well—even making a modest name for myself—and was satisfied with my lot. My oils, watercolors and gouaches had been exhibited, singly and in communal expositions, in several galleries, some of them with a fair amount of luster.

My growing success in my chosen field was due, in no small part, to Janet Lance who was, in the matter of native talent, a near genius. It was Janet who had nurtured my gifts; she had been, in a very real sense, my first teacher. Not only instructing me in the graphic arts, she had been a mentor in other ways. Janet Lance had made me aware of beauty, truth and the metaphysical mysteries. She had come into my life in my formative years and like Pygmalion shaping his clay, had quickened the youthful aspirations in me; Janet had taught me to reach for the stars.

Yet it wasn't Janet who telephoned me on that gray Wednesday in August. It was her husband, Alexander Saxon, calling from the Hotel Carlyle on the Upper East Side of Manhattan. The voice was deep, quiet and rather grave. "Miss Cornwall?" he asked, when I picked up the phone. "How do you do. This is Alexander Saxon, Janet's husband."

It was a dramatic ending to a wild, dark day, a day that had been more like winter than fall, with the temperature hovering in the low thirties and the cold, dank smell of wet stone coming from the sidewalk where the first fat blobs of rain wet the pavement, spattering sharply like the quick cracks of a whip against the asphalt. I had had lunch with a client at one of those dimly-lit, dark-paneled expense account restaurants just east of Fifth Avenue. Young artists don't support themselves on occasional gallery sales; they do illustrations for stories in the glossy magazines, sketch long-limbed ladies with emaciated bodies for department store ads in the newspapers, turn out lettering, posters; in short, pay the rent with their purely commercial efforts.

My business lunch had netted me a remunerative contract. I was to do six color plates and six black and white sketches for the spring catalogue of a mail order house based in Americus, Georgia. The fee was gratifying. I left the restaurant at the end of my three hour lunch and started walking briskly to my brownstone apartment twenty-odd blocks away, a weather eye on

6

the menacing sky and a feeling that if I got home before the deluge started it would be a favorable omen, that it would mean continued good luck. There is a child in all of us, I told myself as I quickened my steps.

By the time I reached my corner the sky had darkened ominously. There was an apocalyptic crash of thunder, followed by a blinding streak of lightning and then the heavens opened, lashing the streets in a tumultuous downpour. Just in time, I thought, and with a congratulatory shake of my shoulders, I ran up the one flight. The telephone was shrilling inside my flat. My keys decided to tangle up, but I was in the house and across the room before the phone stopped ringing.

I picked it up and said hello.

"Miss Cornwall?" a man's voice asked.

"Yes, this is she."

"Hello. This is Alexander Saxon."

I didn't say, *"Who?"* My silence was due only to astonishment. But evidently my caller felt I was at sea, because he added quickly, "Janet's husband."

"Yes, of course. How nice to hear from you, Mr. Saxon."

"I imagine it comes as something of a surprise," he said. "I hope you don't mind. I happened to be in the city and thought it would be—"

"I'm delighted you called me," I said. "Is—"

"Janet's not with me," he cut in, as if he had anticipated my question. "There were some matters I had to attend to, and as a matter of fact I decided to come East at the last minute. It's been a hurried trip."

"I see."

"I . . . uh . . . I realize that it's rather late in the

7

day." There was a brief silence, during which I pictured him consulting a watch or a clock. "Almost four. Yet I wonder if—that is, if you're not otherwise occupied—you'd be kind enough to dine with me this evening. Of course, if you have other plans for the evening—"

I had none. And if I had, would have gone to great pains to cancel them. Janet Lance's husband. Of course I would have dinner with him. I wondered briefly what the person behind the public personality was like, and then said eagerly that I had nothing at all scheduled and would be charmed to see him.

"Wonderful," he said, and then suggested seven thirty as a time to meet, going on to ask me if he might call for me at my apartment.

I said that would be fine. "I'm practically around the corner from the Carlyle, and seven thirty would be agreeable for me."

"Then I'll ring your bell. Is there any place in particular you're fond of? Or would you rather leave it to me?"

I said I'd leave it to him, and we rang off. Seven thirty was three and a half hours away, which left me plenty of time for reminiscences. Janet Lance, I thought. Janet . . .

The years rolled back and there I was, aged eight, my father, victim of a hit and run accident, buried in the cemetery right near the grave of Emily Dickinson. "I'll have to find a job," my mother had said as gently as possible, acquainting me with the new realities of our lives. Mother was a smart little woman and good at figures; in no time at all she was behind a desk at the First National Bank but the salary was small.

Fortunately, our house was large and there were several extra rooms. "I've decided to take in some students from the University," Mother announced next and when the new semester began we had four girls. Mother would never have taken in male boarders; she felt more comfortable with young ladies and a growing daughter was a consideration as well.

My mother's house, I thought . . . where we all lived when we were young, so young . . . my childhood. Our boarding house changed with each Commencement, but of them all, the first to apply for rooms—Norma Perry and Janet Lance—were my favorites and best beloved. Both were tall, dark-haired, with long, swinging legs and large, heavy-lashed eyes. To see the two of them walking along the streets of Amherst, their books in tote bags slung over their broad, handsome shoulders, was a joy. I felt they *belonged* to me. Norma and Janet, I thought it then and I think it still today, were the two loveliest girls on campus. To me they were the Lady of Shalott and Queen Guinevere. They were an inspiration to a developing, fatherless girl and they took me under their wing, making life joyous for me.

Norma had married first. She was now Mrs. Michael Miller, living in Derby, Connecticut. Janet had left La Grange, Illinois, after graduation, putting an end to a difficult, ambivalent relationship with her mother, and had settled on the West Coast. Infrequently, but at least at some kind of regular intervals, Norma still wrote.

Janet?

That was another story. I hadn't heard from Janet for at least six years.

9

Promptly at seven thirty, my bell rang. I pressed the buzzer and footsteps came up the stairs. Tall, slender, every inch the prototype of his publicity photos, Alexander Saxon rounded the bend in the landing. He held out a hand.

I took it and said how nice it was to finally meet Janet's husband. "Please come in. I'm ready, but won't you have a drink before we leave?"

"No, but I would like to be shown round your studio," he said pleasantly. He showed a good deal of interest in my work on drawing board and easel. I watched him as he wandered: if he had not been Janet's husband I would have been curious about him all the same. Alexander Saxon was a name to reckon with in musical circles; he was both composer and conductor, a rising star in his arena. He was still in his mid-thirties and his classical output to date relatively modest—a cantata, an unperformed opera, two tone poems in the manner of Richard Strauss. He was a neo-romantic, eschewing the twelve-tone scale, and was popular in his appearances on the podium (particularly with his female audiences because of his dark good looks).

He came from a wealthy and illustrious New England family and had added to his riches from another source—he wrote background music for films. His name in that field was not especially well-known; the uninitiated are not in the habit of scanning film credits for those behind the scenes. But I knew, because I was in the swing of things, that he earned large sums of money from the movie scores he ground out . . . and he had done at least a dozen of those.

10

We finally left my apartment and taxied to the Copenhagen. It was odd, but all the while we were sipping cocktails I didn't feel that I was with Janet Lance's husband. I felt only that I was with Alexander Saxon, composer and conductor. I suppose I couldn't get past the fact of his reputation. Public personalities acquire a kind of facade, like varnish, and although at one point he said easily, "Oh, do call me Alex, and may I call you Kip," it was not until he came to the reason for his contacting me that, almost guiltily, I remembered that this attractive and faintly intimidating man was the husband of an old friend.

I had just asked him if he was going to be in Manhattan for long. "No, I'm flying back tomorrow," he said. "I came only for the week."

It occurred to me that this meeting might be purely duty, that Janet had asked him to please look up her friend Kip Cornwall, do something nice for her and give her her love. This rather defensive reaction was, however, dispelled a second later when he said, "I'm very glad you could see me tonight, you know, because there's a particular favor I wanted to ask from you. It may seem ridiculous, in view of the fact that you're so much younger . . ."

He gave me a quick, comprehensive look and asked if I would have another drink. When I said no, he asked if I minded if *he* had another one. When it came, he scarcely touched it after the first sip. Our small talk lagged, and a sixth sense told me that he had wanted to delay dinner until he had gotten whatever it was he wanted to ask me off his mind. He reached for his cigarettes and pulled one out. Then he

11

lit it and only when he puffed quickly on it and set it down in the ashtray did he notice that he already had a half-finished one burning there.

He shook his head, frowned, and then lifted his shoulders in a wry shrug. "I'm really quite normal in other ways," he said, by way of explanation, and of course I laughed and said we all did things like that when we had something on our minds.

"I suppose so," he answered. "And yes, I do have something on my mind. That's why I wanted to ask this favor of you, Kip." His quiet smile came again and he interrupted himself. "Do you mind," he said. "I find myself resisting calling you Kip. Is it short for something?"

"Yes, of course. It's Katherine."

"That's much better," he said. "You won't object if I call you that instead?"

"I've outgrown Kip by a half dozen years," I assured him. "Please say Katherine."

"Then Katherine," he said, "I'll explain what this is all about. I'm more than a little worried about Janet."

"Why?"

He studied his cigarette. "She isn't sick, her health's quite robust, though she has that ethereal look." His quick smile came again. "When I first met her I told her she looked like a quattrocento madonna. She liked that very much."

"I always said she was like a Burne-Jones. Or any of the pre-Raphaelites."

He nodded. "The point is, she's from another era. One doesn't simply label Janet a pretty woman. It would be a vapid thing to say. It comes naturally to use hyperbole."

"I know what you mean."

"But," he added, with another smile, "I digress. I simply thought that, if you can manage to spare the time, you might write her once in a while. Without being too obvious. Just an occasional note."

"Yes, I'd certainly love to do that," I agreed. "I'd *adore* hearing from her. You see, I've always felt I owed so much to Jan." I was beginning to warm to the idea. "Suppose I say I met you, and that it was very pleasant and—"

"Don't say you met me," he interrupted quickly. "Better not."

"Oh?" I was understandably taken aback.

"No reason to . . . she might . . ."

He fell silent again.

"Okay," I said, becoming more and more puzzled. And then I was quite blunt about it. "Hasn't Janet any close friends out there?"

"Not really. She paints, spends a good deal of time in her studio. And there are the children." He crushed out his cigarette and then went on. "Of course there are her parents as well."

"Her parents?" I sat up attentively. "Are they visiting?"

"No no. They've moved out near us."

Oh, my Lord, I thought. Oh, poor Janet. Her parents out there *with* her? "I had no idea," I said aloud.

"Yes, they have a beautiful small house not far from ours. I enjoy them very much. Caroline is such a brilliant pianist. She should certainly have done concert work."

"Yes, she plays wonderfully well," I said dryly. "Well, then, I'll just find some item of interest for Jan

13

and send it on with a little note. When we used to correspond, years ago, we sent enclosures. Things that struck a common chord. I could do that."

"That sounds splendid," he said. "I trust you to handle it well. It's very good of you, Katherine."

He seemed about to dismiss the subject and I saw him looking toward the waiter, but I just couldn't let it go at that. Persistently, I said, "If you aren't worried about Jan's health in any way, why *are* you worried, Alex?"

He looked at me and away again. Then, without glancing back and with his eyes attentively on the opposite wall, he murmured, "It has crossed my mind, in particularly dark moments of the soul, that my wife might be losing her mind."

I heard my own indrawn breath, felt the color draining from my face. "Oh, no," I whispered. "You can't really mean that."

He turned and faced me directly. "And now that I've said it, I don't believe a word of it," he said almost cheerfully. "You're to forget what I just said, Katherine, and never think of it again. Perhaps I said it only to test myself. To see how saying it would affect me. In any case, it was an unforgivable thought to voice to someone who is a stranger to me and a good friend to the person in question. You see, I love my wife. I'm concerned about my private, personal world and I sense that there is something wrong. But it isn't *that,* I'm sure."

He gave me a quick, encompassing glance. "I suppose too," he said, "that I took my cue from you yourself. I think I have a feeling about people, and I sense a maturity in you, young as you are. *I'm* no longer

14

really young, but you are. Just the same, in spite of the fact that you look almost a child, with that flyaway, shoulder-length hair and that candid, ungarnished face, you're—"

He crushed out another cigarette.

"May I add, a very lovely, sensitive face."

I didn't feel self-conscious; Jan's husband didn't make me react that way. His compliment was friendly and I knew what I was like: healthy and tanned and lightly freckled. Nature had given me all my arms and legs and a not too unprepossessing appearance . . . and a conscience.

"I think we should have something to eat," Alex said, and held his hand up for the waiter.

It was almost eleven when I was dropped off outside my brownstone.

"I've enjoyed this very much," Alex said, taking my hand. "I hope it's been as pleasant for you."

"Yes it has," I said.

"You'll write Janet?"

"Of course."

"Thank you."

He said he would wait until I was inside, and he did. Rounding the bend of the stairs, I could see him still standing there, through the glass doors at the bottom, patiently waiting until he saw me safely out of sight.

Falling asleep I remembered, troubled, the words he had told me to forget.

I think my wife is losing her mind.

But I was tired, and I fell asleep soon afterwards.

And next morning the shock had lessened. When you loved someone you imagined all sorts of things. It

15

was *that* Alex was plagued by . . . love and concern and deep involvement.

That was all it was. Nothing more than that.

And so I started a correspondence with Janet. I began by sending her a brochure from a gallery showing of mine, and shortly afterwards she wrote back. "I knew you'd make it," she said in her note. "How exciting, Kip. I want you to know how happy I am."

Other answers followed other letters of mine and for a short while there was a regular flow between us. I found myself looking forward, eagerly, to my California mail and on those days when there was an envelope from Janet, flew back upstairs to my flat, with an anticipatory nail ripping open the flap.

And then, abruptly, Janet's letters stopped coming. I kept on with my end of it. But it was no use. Janet simply didn't answer.

At Christmas time, however, I had a card with a group family snapshot enclosed. Janet, looking beautiful with a silver streak in her hair, sat with two adorable little boys at her knee. Alex, tall and impressive, stood behind her. I acknowledged this with a photo of myself and sat back to wait. I felt sure that a picture of "the little girl grown up" would elicit a response.

But there was only silence.

I had, by this time, become obsessed with thoughts of Janet. I couldn't seem to shake off my uneasy feelings about her. Norma, from whom I heard spasmodically, could be of little help at the moment: she was again pregnant, nearing term, and unfortunately plagued with a toxic condition which made her feel miserable. Nothing dangerous, at least with proper

16

care and rest, but I felt I couldn't add to her problems. So I didn't voice my uneasiness about Janet.

February went by and then March, and in late April I came down with bronchial pneumonia. Respiratory infections have a depressing effect and I found myself, with nothing to do but try to get well, brooding endlessly about Janet. Why didn't I hear from her? Why the enthusiastic spate of letters last fall and winter and then nothing? And why (I must confess it hurt quite a bit) hadn't she acknowledged my snapshot?

I found myself dreaming about her. Sometimes gentle, warm dreams, with the feel of her arms around me . . . and at other times dark, vague dreams, the meaning of which eluded me.

I couldn't get Janet off my mind. She had been, if you will, a happy memory for a good many years. Then suddenly, with the unexpected appearance of her husband last year, had become vivid to me once more. I kept thinking about how much I owed her. It was mainly due to Janet Lance that I had made my way safely through the thickets and brambles of what would otherwise have been a difficult adolescence. Half orphaned and with a working mother who had her own griefs and problems, I had turned to Janet for guidance. She had been there when I needed someone . . . which had been often.

When I was up and around again I got out the snapshot that had come at holiday time. Janet was so lovely-looking, with that silver streak at her widow's peak. Perhaps art, perhaps nature; it didn't matter. Janet Saxon was still, would always be I was sure, a vibrantly beautiful woman. I looked long at the fine-boned face, the high, intelligent forehead, and

17

then made up my mind. For once in my cautious, industrious life I could do something impulsive. Being a free-lance artist meant you could come and go as you pleased. And right now, tomorrow if possible, it was Katherine Cornwall's pleasure to go to California.

I called the airline, found that I could book a flight for the morning after the following one and then, with a feeling of almost unbearable anticipation, put through a person to person call to Big Sur.

Inside of half an hour I was speaking to Janet.

Her voice sounded different. Higher, quicker.

"Yes," she said, a little impatiently. "Who is this?"

"Jan, it's Kip."

There was a brief, buzzing silence. Then, "Kip?"

Just that. Just my name, with a question mark, as if she were in doubt about who Kip was.

"Janet? It's Katherine Cornwall. Your obedient correspondent." I felt let down, aware of an empty feeling in the pit of my stomach. "Am I calling at a bad time?"

"No no! Oh, my Lord, it's Kip," she said, and warmth suddenly rushed into her voice. "Dear *child,* what are you *doing* spending your money on transcontinental telephone calls? How *are* you? I've loved your letters."

"I've loved yours," I said. "It's wonderful to be talking to you."

Brave words: the fact was that my first flush of determination was waning. I didn't really want to give myself time to think. I wanted to get out there, to see her. I didn't want anything to stop me. But talking to her now, especially with that first impatient, preoccupied greeting, I was suddenly conscious of how time and circumstance had parted us. I could picture, as I had never really pictured before, her life, of which I knew only the rudimentary details . . . her house, her children, her servants, friends, acquaintances.

People who were all part of Janet's life, a Janet I didn't know. The girl I had loved didn't really exist any more. That girl had lived in another time, another place . . . frozen forever in the memory of those of us who had known her then.

"Imagine you calling like this," she said, and suddenly it sounded like Janet again, the old Janet with the rich contralto voice, the voice like warm sherry, like sweet honey. "How exciting, Kip! Are you doing well, then?"

"Yes, in fact I've been working so hard I think I need a vacation."

"Oh? Where will you go?"

"Somewhere," I said, and then thought, I don't care how long it's been or whether we're two different people from what we used to be. This was Janet, after all. This was Janet.

"I've never been to California," I said. "I thought I might go there."

There was a long, weird silence. Too long. This time my heart sank clear down to my knees. She didn't want me to come. That was clear. All too clear.

Then her voice came on again. "Why not?" she asked, in a kind of abstracted way, as if she were talking to herself. "Why not?" she repeated softly. "Oh, Kip, do come! Come and stay with me! God, imagine seeing you again after all this time. Imagine! Like old times."

I picked at the edge of my desk blotter. "I only

meant to stop and say hello when I was out there," I said slowly . . . and dishonestly. "Of course I'd love to see you, but—"

"Don't be idiotic! I'll get a room ready for you. We have more space than we know what to do with. Kip, I'm expecting you!"

"Do you really want to see me?" I asked.

"I do, I do! How can you say that? Will it be soon?"

"It could be any time. Right away, for that matter. I've called for a booking. I could take a flight in the morning, day after tomorrow."

"Take it. Get on that plane, promise me? What time does it leave New York?" She made an impatient sound. "When do you arrive *here?*"

"I get into San Francisco, your time, at noon. I should be away from the airport and in the city not too long after that."

"Okay, let's see. Suppose I meet you, say about one thirty, at the Fairmont? Take a cab from the airport, tell him the Hotel Fairmont. Just wait in the lounge and I'll find you."

"You're sure it's all right? Not an inconvenient time?"

"No. At first I thought . . . but it doesn't matter. Nothing matters. Just seeing you will do me a world of good. I must rush right away and look at the photo you sent me. You looked very pretty in that."

"It was somewhat flattering," I said. "But anyway, I'm tall. As tall as you are, I expect. I stand five foot nine. I'm a monster, in fact. It's difficult with men. You remember."

"Lord, yes. Those blind dates were always pigmies." A giggle came over the wires, the giggle of the Janet of old. "Oh, Kip, whatever you do, don't miss that plane."

"All right, I won't."

"This is a particularly good time. It will be a long, lazy summer. Alex won't be on tap until the fall, when he'll go to London to conduct the Halle Orchestra and then on to Munich. But he's completely free for the time being. So you see?"

"Well, then, if you're sure it's all right."

"All right? It's the nicest thing that's happened to me in a long, long time."

After we rang off I thought about that last sentence. *The nicest thing that's happened to me in a long, long time.* It was such a strange thing to say: an affluent woman, beautiful, protected, with a notable husband and two lovely children. What more could anyone want?

Yet in the most quintessential beauty there could be a flaw. An imperfection, like the blemish at the heart of an otherwise perfect diamond, coarsening an outwardly sublime loveliness, making it second rate, paltry, meretricious.

There was something wrong in Janet's life, I thought, as I packed my bags. Something hidden, obscure . . . something that was eating at her . . . and which, ultimately, could destroy her.

Imagination? Hysteria? Possibly. But just the same it was the reason for my going to her, and at the last moment I called Norma, whose baby was now a few months old. When I told her what had been going on, she was questioning too, though at first she thought I was making too much of it. "Still, it can't hurt to go out and see," she said, in her crisp, efficient way. If it's all in your mind you'll soon find out. Meanwhile you'll have a vacation out of it."

Ten minutes after we had said good-bye the phone rang. It was Norma.

"I've been thinking," she said. "And let's put it this way, Kip. You're not an alarmist. If it seems to you that something might be amiss, you may be right. I just wanted to say, let me know what you can when you can. Call me if at all possible. Make it person to person collect and don't worry about the cost. Mike's over the twenty thousand a year hump and we can afford it. Just keep me posted if you find out anything. You must promise."

"All right," I said, out of habit crossing my heart, as the three of us had once done.

"And godspeed. The baby is crying. I must go, but remember, if you're troubled, I'm here, at this end. Let me know what's going on there."

"Yes, Norma."

I was at the airport ridiculously early. But then I was anxious to get there. I hoped the gifts I had hastily purchased would please Jan's two little boys, and I hoped too that the Lanvin scarf I had bought Jan would make her happy.

Janet had always prized quality things.

Over a glass of champagne, airborne, I was thinking: it's been a long time, a very long time. We were no longer blithe and carefree, who once were so hauntingly young . . .

Chapter 2

As it happened, my flight was almost half an hour early on arrival. I was at the Fairmont at a little before one. Janet had said one thirty in the lobby, but I half expected her to be already there and waiting for me. Wishful thinking; she was not, and I sat there for a short while, feeling the minutes drag. After a bit, unable to sit still a second longer, I got up and went over to ask the desk clerk where the coffee shop was.

He indicated the direction and added that the taproom lay just beyond. As soon as he said taproom I decided that a brandy would calm me and help me get rid of my case of jitters. Yes, jitters; those years of old seemed very far away at this moment in time, and I felt unaccountably shy.

I sat down in a corner of the pine-paneled room. There was a buzz of talk and laughter, and I ordered a sandwich with my drink. The drink came first and, lighting a cigarette, I sipped, glancing about idly. And in doing so, to my immense surprise and pleasure, caught sight of Janet on the other side of the room.

So she *had* arrived early!

Janet had been eager for our meeting too. I put down my glass, primed to get up and wave. How lovely she looked, how cool and dark and soignee . . . she had on a sleeveless dress of lettuce-green. Her hair was caught high at the crown of her head and from there it cascaded down in a luxuriant mass of glossy black. Her face, from this distance, seemed smooth and unlined and my heart leapt with gratitude. The years had been kind to Janet's beauty.

I was half out of my seat when I suddenly noticed that Janet wasn't alone but was seated with a companion at a banquette for two. I promptly sat down again, and the reason for my doing so was that the person Janet was with was not another woman but a man. Not only that, but the two of them were deeply engrossed in a conversation, so much so that the word which came to my mind was "rendezvous." Because, sitting there side by side, looking into each other's eyes and with hands touching on the table top, it would have been evident to anyone that this was no casual encounter between acquaintances, or even old friends. They were so totally absorbed in each other that, even if I had been at a nearby table, I doubt if Jan would have seen me. My impression was that there was only one person in that room she was really aware of, and that was the man next to her.

However, aside from that, there was almost the whole room between us. And as I nibbled my sandwich and sipped my drink, I studied the man Janet was with, furtively, and with an interest which was only quite natural. It was his hair that struck me at first, hair that was like pale fire, like a gold ingot. His face? There was something timeless about it, as there was about Janet's, something reminiscent of another century, another time. He had the fine, chiseled bones and dark, deep-set eyes (contrasting with his fair hair) of a painting by Giotto or Ingres.

He was, roughly, in his late thirties and, even sitting down, I could tell that he was taller than average.

It really seemed idiotic not to get up and go over to Janet, I thought, when I had finished my sandwich and drained my glass. I signaled my waiter, he brought my check and I settled my bill. I looked over to where my friend was sitting, and made up my mind. Of course I would go over. Of course.

I picked up my change, left the usual twenty percent for the waiter and scraped back my chair.

And at that precise moment Janet's companion picked up both of her hands, held them for a moment, and then put one of them to his lips.

And Janet?

She closed her eyes for a moment, then opened them again and bent to put her cheek to the temple of the man beside her. I couldn't hear what was said, but I could see her whispering something.

I, of course, changed my mind.

I got up quickly, made my way through the nest of tables near me, and with a quick backward glance, went out through the glass doors again, lugging my suitcase. As I glanced over my shoulder, I saw that I hadn't been spotted.

Janet saw only one person. The man at her side.

About ten minutes later, she came through the front entrance, saw me sitting there, and rushed forward.

25

"Hello, Kip *darling*," she cried, arms outstretched, and her cheek met mine as I got up to meet her embrace. The well-remembered fragrance of her enveloped me . . . perhaps not still Arpege, but something very like it. "Well, you *are* a big girl," she said, holding me off. "I just can't believe it."

"Yes, I shot up," I said. "I warned you about that."

"Goodness, yes. How groovy, terrific, this is. Okay, let's get going. We have time for a little sight-seeing before driving back. Not *too* much time, but don't worry. You'll be seeing plenty of San Francisco in the days to come. We live in a beautiful area, but there's a car for you, and you'll get tired of the beach in short order. It's not all that long a drive from country to city."

She drove me all about: Lombard Street, zigzagging down from a great height, a fabulous street in a surrounding area of nothing very much, Washington and Union Squares, the Mission Dolores with its old, old graves, Nob Hill, the Twin Peaks, Hyde and Joyce Streets, the former with its cable car and the latter in a very old-world section, Golden Gate Park where, astonishingly, there was a statue of Goethe and Schiller on a single pedestal, and of course Fisherman's Wharf, where we stopped off and had a Brandy Alexander.

It was a diamond-bright city until about three in the afternoon, when the fog settled down, swathing the buildings. The Presidio, barely glimpsed through swarming foliage, was also further obscured by the mist, and on the observation deck where we parked for a distance view of the Golden Gate bridge, the shadowy white curtain bathed us in a wet mist when we got out and stood eyeing the magnificent rust-red

26

structure that stretched, a surrealistic span, across the bay, dream-spun, imaginative, thrilling. Salty and scent-drenched, with its pungent smells, it was, I thought, like being at the very bottom of the sea. And then, gazing up at the superlative view of the clambering city, I thought of a poem by Coleridge.

> In Xanadu did Kubla Khan
> A stately pleasure-dome decree:
> Where Alph, the sacred river ran
> Through caverns measureless to man
> Down to a sunless sea . . .

I told Janet what I was thinking.

"Odd you should say that," she murmured. "Our house is called Xanadu."

She shrugged. "Silly name, isn't it? But then, it's a silly house."

At a place called Ghiradelli Square, a very pretty little section at the foot of the city and with a waterfront view, Janet said she wanted to stop off. "There's a book store for children. I always bring the boys something."

She was unable to find a parking space and so she asked me to wait in the car for her. "I'll hurry," she promised.

But she was gone for quite a long time. And then a policeman came and poked his head in the window. "You can't stay here," he said politely but firmly.

"My friend will be right out," I told him. She just went into one of the shops."

"I'm sorry, you'll have to move."

"But it's not my car."

27

"You can drive, can't you?"

"Yes, but—"

"Then, please," he said. "You'll have to leave this spot. Just circle the square and pick your friend up when she comes out."

There was no alternative. I slid over, put the car in gear, and pulled away. I drove round the square from Bay Street, which was where Janet had left me, round to Beach Street at the opposite end of the square and back to Bay Street again.

Janet wasn't there yet. And the cop caught my eye. He shook his head and I drove round again.

It was a very pretty square, though rather spoiled at the south end by a super-modern, garish development not in keeping with the rest of its character. But even this compound was beautifully planned, with a lovely little park on the river side and small, attractive shops, including a cheerful-looking bistro on the corner of Beach and Larkin Streets. In fact it was all so appealing that I was not at all averse to making my second turn around, noting the Cannery to the north, a winsome Little Theatre just above it, and another isty bitsy park at the left of some very attractive row houses just across from my original starting place.

The row houses—brick, several stories high—were very handsome, much like the East Side brown or limestone townhouses of Manhattan. The green of old trees lined the sidewalk in front of them. I thought idly that living in one of them, in this charming setting, would be very nice. This was just as I was about to make my third circumlocution. And as I started on my peripatetic way again, I spotted, with a start of surprise, the man I had seen with Janet at the hotel.

28

Why, that's him, I thought, idling the motor.

And it was, no doubt about it. I saw first his blond, bright head and his height and then, inching along as slowly as the traffic would allow, I followed his progress. He was walking briskly along the street and then he turned into one of the row houses on the north side of Bay Street.

He went up the walk, climbed four stone steps and let himself in the front door.

It was at that point that I began wondering. About Janet. And about that man.

You sensed some things. And *I* sensed, not wanting to think it but unable not to, that Janet was having an affair.

"I always take the boys something from this little shop."

Always?

Whenever she drove into San Francisco . . . to see that man.

And I knew, at that moment, that the picture was resolving in my mind. I hadn't been born yesterday. Women did these things. And it looked as if Janet was doing it. Was seeing this man on and off.

Oh, dear.

I tried not to think further about it, but I had a vision of Janet, escaping from her Big Sur house and coming into San Francisco on certain days in the week, going to that house on Bay Street . . . spending a day, a half day, a few hours. Disappearing into an unknown part of her life.

Troubled and disheartened, I completed my third turn and this time Janet was standing there, tapping her foot.

"What happened?" she asked, when I stopped the car.

"No parking, it seems," I said. "An officer told me to—"

"What officer, where is he?"

I opened the door so she could get in, and slid over to the right hand seat. She climbed inside and took a deep, furious breath. "Is that the man?" she asked, pointing.

The policeman who had spoken to me was only a few yards away. "Yes," I said. "But, Jan, what does it matter? You have to have some kind of rules and regulations."

"Damn these petty bureaucrats," she said furiously. "They're not paid to badger you, how dare they?"

The policeman came abreast of us.

Janet leaned out the window and beckoned to him. "Officer, are you trying to harass us?" she demanded. "I was only gone for a very short while. My friend is from New York and she was waiting in the car. Couldn't you have stretched a point? My car was not left unattended. What do you have to gain by—"

The man looked bewildered. "Ma'am?" he said, and then recognized me. He came up to us and put a hand on the side of the car. "There are signs, no parking," he pointed out.

"For a few stupid *minutes*," Janet said angrily. "With all that's going on in this rotten world. Yes, and I'll remember this when I pay my taxes. Such pettiness. And everything you read in the newspapers—the Supreme Court riddled with dishonest judges, the student outrages . . ."

She slapped the wheel with an imperious hand.

"Give me a ticket, then," she said loudly. "I demand that you give me a ticket. I'm waiting, officer."

Transfixed, I caught the patrolman's eye. Please, my eyes pleaded with his. Let us go. Take into consideration that this woman is upset . . . and let us go.

The man, who was clearly a human being, decided in favor of us. "I'm sorry, Ma'am," he said quietly. "Just get going, if you don't mind, and there'll be no trouble."

"Oh yes," Janet said stridently and then suddenly, like air going out of a swollen balloon, her incomprehensible spleen evaporated. She put a hand over her eyes and then leaned back. Her smile was wry and even amused. "Oh, dear," she said contritely. "Don't take me to jail. I promise to mend my manners. May we go?"

The cop was visibly relieved. He stepped back.

Janet pulled away with a hand uplifted in a parting salute. *"Ciao,"* she called and then drove away. In another minute we were on the Expressway. "We'll be home before seven," Janet said. "We won't eat until around nine, maybe a bit later, so that will give us all time to relax over drinks on the terrace. There are cigarettes in the compartment there. Can you find them? It will be a dreary drive until we get to Santa Cruz, and after that we'll have some scenery."

"Okay, Jan," I said, and craned my neck to get a last view of the Golden Gate bridge. But there wasn't much to see. Almost all of it was shrouded by the fog.

Chapter 3

Perhaps to cover up her discomfiture at her outburst with the street policeman, Janet talked incessantly on the ride. "California's so *sameish*," she complained. "I sometimes long for snow, for New England winters." She peered at me in the rear view mirror. "You know, when you were little I wasn't sure you'd turn out pretty. I knew you'd be pleasant-looking with that up-turned mouth and those amiable eyes. But I can see now that you have wonderful bone structure, Kip. Now that the chipmunk cheeks are gone, the formless baby face defined and structured."

"I'm glad you're *not* too disappointed, Janet."

"I'm pleased, very pleased. I shall find time to paint you. We're a bit alike, you know. Not in our features, but our build. That's interesting, isn't it?"

A fleeting wistfulness crossed her face. "You know, since I've been hearing from you again, I've been thinking that you were, in a way, the first of my children. I was really fond of you, Kip. I don't think you ever really knew how fond."

"I loved you better than anyone," I said simply, feeling disloyal, because I knew it was true that, even more than my mother, I had given most of my love to Janet in those early years.

"Is your apartment nice, Kip?"

"It's a studio, actually. I tell people I don't work where I live. I live where I work. It's . . . well, cluttered. But yes, it's got wonderful light, high ceilings and a working fireplace. I'm very comfortable there."

"Wonderful. You're happy, then."

"Sometimes."

"And doing well. So you see how things work out. Your talent paid off."

"Due to you."

"To me?"

"Of course, it's true, Jan. You got me started. I was all tight at first. Remember? You said, 'Kip, get out of that tiny little corner and fill the damned canvas!' You took my hand and the charcoal screeched across the Watman board."

"I nagged, did I?"

"You were . . ." I started to say "merciless," but amended it. "You were great. A marvelous teacher."

"You had it in you. I could see that. I wanted you to get out of that small *town*. Not get buried there. That dear, silly, bourgeois little mother of yours. Respectability at any price. So I did help you?"

"It's why I'm doing what I'm doing. Because you made me."

"That's nice."

I didn't for a minute think she was on drugs. But

34

she was *like* that. Edgy, big-eyed, vague, somehow. And that crack about my mother . . . Yes, of course, Mother had been all for the orderly things of life; to be nice, to be good and proper. Well, that was another generation. But the thing was, Janet had been so *good* to her. Bringing her a box of Barton's truffles every Friday night, buying asters for the table. Janet had been so gentle with Mother. I remembered, and I hadn't thought about this for years, a letter she had written after my mother had given a birthday party for her. The next day the letter was lying at my mother's place at the breakfast table.

Dear Good Lady:
Thank you for that spiffy, beautiful party. Lucky, lucky me. To have such a good lady providing for me. The cake was out of sight and I'll save the candles forever. You're the best I ever knew. Thanks, soulful thanks and kisses, love, eternally. My dear, dear friend.

They had yakked together for hours. Not Norma. Just Janet. Mother and Janet. Sometimes I had felt like a stepchild. But I always thought, never mind, let Mother have Janet. She had so little else.

"How's Norma?" Janet asked, her hands on the wheel, loosely.

"Fine. Domestic. Child-bearing. The two of you. Doing women's things. Me? I'm still the struggling career girl."

"How about men?"

"They're around. No one I've fallen madly for."

She laughed shortly. "Domestic . . . me? Oh, dear.

35

Hardly that. I let the help cope. I'm generally paint-stained and unpresentable. Will that taint my children, will they grow up to lie on the analyst's couch? I find life very difficult, Kip. I haven't decided, to date, whether it's worth living. What do you think?"

It was said in a lightly conversational tone. But people don't voice thoughts like that just for fun. You either enjoyed or you didn't. You either wanted to get up in the morning or you didn't.

"I think it is," I said, trying not to sound crass. I meant it. I thought it was splendid to be alive.

There was a quite long silence. And then, rounding a turn in the road, she asked, "Are the onion fields still there?"

"Yes, Jan."

The onion fields . . .

You came to a junction, where four roads met. Hadley was one way, Amherst another. Southampton was to the west and Holyoke to the east. And stretching out, between the four points of these townships, were the onion fields.

That pungent smell at the crossroads . . .

In the rear view mirror I saw her eyes, dark, beautiful, fathomless. So she remembered.

"That was a hell of a long time ago," she said, and went on talking. Chattering, rather, and she smoked continuously, lighting a cigarette from the butt of another. I noticed that her hands, which were constantly in motion—gesturing, putting her cigarette to her mouth and then jerking it away—shook every so slightly. It was *almost* imperceptible, but if you knew her, had known her before, it was impossible not to note it.

36

She was also driving at a high rate of speed. The gauge registered eighty miles an hour. The shrubbery at the side of the road was whizzing by, and I couldn't help thinking, *if a tire blew* . . .

"You're going like a bat out of hell," I observed.

"It's a clear road," she said, but eased up on the gas a trifle, and then lit another cigarette.

Small things, little things. Things most people wouldn't see at all. And although it was coming to me slowly and in little pieces, there was the feeling of being with a stranger. Yes, she was talking about old times, recalling a long-ago past. The recollections were vivid, but the person sitting next to me was almost an impostor.

The Janet I had known had been a quiet, restful person. It was Norma who had been the vocal one, vivacious, loquacious. A little wild. She and Janet had complemented each other because of their personality differences. But this Janet was far more frenetic, more reckless, more brittle. This woman had changed, from the old Janet to a new one.

Was this what the years did to a person?

Or was I simply looking for signs? Was it only because Alex had said what he had? I was conscious of an unpleasant idea. I glanced at Janet, studied her furtively, and then looked quickly away. A case history, I thought. It was as if I were a psychologist and Janet my subject. I had the cold, weird notion that I was analyzing someone for scientific purposes, that everything Janet said and did was being registered on a hidden tape recorder.

It was a horrid feeling and I had a quick surge of anger, blaming Janet's husband. It was he who made

37

me question every look and expression of my friend's, he who had put ideas into my head.

I thought with regret, I shouldn't have come. Suddenly I wanted very much to be back in my studio-apartment with its north light, sitting at my drawing board or standing at my easel, deep in my very own, private life.

But I was *here,* and the Monterey peninsula was beautiful after a given point, with its shore drive, its twisted pines crippled by the forces of land and sea gales, its shimmering expanse of sea blue and glittering in the sun. "We're just about home," Janet said finally. "You'll either like our house or you'll hate it. Alex says it's a rum sort of place but we wouldn't be there except for him. He picked it out. We rent it from a former movie siren of the silents. She's troubled by arthritis and one presumes cirrhosis of the liver due to a strong taste for the grape. In short, she's an old lush. I'm fond of her; we see her occasionally and pay her an enormous monthly stipend."

A minute later, rising above the rest of the scenery and atop a cliff, was Xanadu. I had just seen Victorian houses in San Francisco, but I had never expected to see one here, in Big Sur. I had anticipated a very large, A-frame house with peaked roofs and great glass walls, contemporary and suited to the seaside. A glorified beach house, in fact.

It was nothing like that. It was like the tremendous old houses at Southampton or Newport, only more so. It looked a little bit like the Kremlin, with the most fantastic architectural embellishments imaginable; it was sheer Byzantine. There was a round, crenellated turret, a double-domed cupola, three minarets of vary-

38

ing shapes, was three-storied under its fancy gabling and on the second story a veranda ran full-length, all trimmed in lacy-work. It was gray-painted frame, but one of the domes was gilded, catching, in the blaze of fire, the light from the sun.

I was dazzled. "It's fantastic," I said, gazing. "*This* is where you live?"

"It was originally supposed to be temporary," she said, grinning. "But here we are, after all these years." She turned up a road and then cut the motor and we sat there for another minute. There was a silence and yet not a silence. There was a profound sense of peace, of isolation, yet this was broken by the pounding of the sea down below, by the cries of gulls, the swish of leaves in the trees as the wind swept the lonely coast . . . and over and above these sounds of nature, something else.

It was music, and it came from the house.

"They're at it again," Janet said. "Mother and Alex."

"Your mother?" I feigned surprise, feeling dishonest and a little cheap. "Your parents are visiting too?"

"No, not visiting. They live here."

"Oh?"

"They've a house very near to us."

I braced myself; now Janet would say something angry and bitter . . . *I put a continent between myself and Mother and now she's here, right under my nose.*

But she didn't say anything like that. Quite the contrary. She said, "It's very nice, you know. Alex has another pair of hands with which to make music."

I was dumbfounded. Janet, for as long as I had known her, had been at war with her mother. Yet here

39

she was, mildly telling me that the status quo was "very nice."

Would wonders never cease?

We got out of the car and she indicated a cluster of other cars: a red Mustang, a bright blue Triumph and a sporty orange Porsche. The car Janet had been driving was a small, sand-colored Dauphine. "Yes, and you're to avail yourself of one of these," she said, catching my glance at them. "This one's my favorite, if you don't mind, Kip, and Alex likes the Porsche. But as to the rest, take your choice."

She pulled my suitcase out of the back seat and we walked across a rough but very green lawn. "Welcome to Xanadu," Janet said, and pushed open the front door.

And so I walked into Janet Lance Saxon's house and into her life as it was now. I was thinking that everything was very, very different from what I had envisioned. What I had envisioned was the young, untried Janet of the old days. The young girl I had once known. But the years had gone by. What had been was long ago.

I had no way of knowing that, way back in the fall of last year, when Alexander had made that phone call to me, it had started a chain of circumstances that was now inevitable.

Chapter 4

The music surged round us as we entered the house, a house which I was soon to to find was filled with many lives and many destinies. I met them all in varying stages: first Jan's two little boys, Alex Junior and Roger. It was Roger who asked me with an eagerness I found gratifying and comforting how many days I was staying. I said I really didn't know.

"A hundred days?" he asked. "A thousand days?"

It sounded poetic and I told him so. "It makes me think of *Anne of The Thousand Days*," I said.

"What's that?" Alex Junior asked curiously, leaning up against me.

"It's a play. About Anne Boleyn. She was married to King Henry the Eighth. And they were married for a thousand days."

"And then what happened?"

"Tragedy," I said. "It was very sad."

"I like sad things," the older boy said. "Sad things make you think."

41

Precocious, I mused, but I should have guessed it, with two highly talented parents. "Think right now about going to bed," Janet said matter of factly, and told me that they had been permitted to wait up for me. "You'll see Kip tomorrow," she said to them.

All the while the music was pouring through the house, a euphony of cadenzas and apogiaturas. It came from a room off the entrance hall, with closed doors, very old-fashioned, pulled together, which did little to diminish the sounds . . . but then Liszt was never noted for being a quietly lyrical composer. It was all very gorgeous, a waterfall of sound. ("And fury," a critic of Liszt's day is reputed to have penned. "Signifying nothing.")

"Let them finish in there," Janet said, looking toward the closed doors. "I wouldn't dare interrupt them." She put her arms around her two children, told them that now they had met her friend Kip it was time to turn in. "I want her to come up and say good-night to us," Roger said, sticking out his chin.

"Tomorrow. But not tonight. And no protests. *Comprends?*"

"But Mother . . ."

"Up with you."

The two children trudged up the stairs, with longing backward glances. Janet nudged them ahead and I was left alone.

I sat down on the bottom step, listening to the music and was leaning against the banister with my eyes closed when I heard a voice. I jumped; I hadn't heard anyone approach.

"This is Janet's friend?"

I opened my eyes to see a man past middle age

standing in front of me. He was broad, stocky and in spite of his medium stature was powerfully built.

I started to get up but he stopped me and sat himself down next to me. "I'm Zoltan," he said. His voice was accented, very thick and middle European. He had a big head with a high, bony, intellectual forehead, and his eyes were alert and intelligent. "Listen," he said, with a glance up the stairs.

I had already heard it. Janet was singing a lullaby. Her rich contralto drifted down.

"And are you goin' to Scarborough Fair . . ."

Remembering, I thought of Janet and Norma, in close harmony, their young voices raised in song.

Scarlet ribbons in her hair . . .

"My mother," the stranger said, "used to sing the Kreisler tune. *How swiftly, silently, the moments fly . . . till years like winging birds go quickly by . . ."*

"My mother didn't sing anything," I said. "She had other duties."

"A pity. Lullabies are for children what tranquilizers are for adults."

"You're right, I expect. But my mother was widowed early and the poor thing didn't have much time for sentiment."

"Again I'm sorry," he said. "Are you wondering who I am?"

I laughed. He was a singular personality, even at first flush, and I took to him immediately.

"Of course you are wondering. All right. But first let me brief you on the others. There are three of us here, outside the family. The Japanese boy, the young violin student and myself. We exist on the bounty of the Saxons."

43

"Oh?"

"But," he said, "the two children have something to sell. That is to say, my young friend, they are investments of a kind. You know what an investment is?"

He waited, and I could see he was a prolix old gentleman and plainly full of himself. "An investment is a gamble," I answered. "You can lose your money but on the other hand you can double it."

He seemed pleased with my answer. "Exactly. And now let me explain, please. Tony—he's the Japanese boy, Tony Jung—is a brilliant protégé of Mr. Saxon's. He studies composition with Mr. Saxon, who thinks he will one day be a great modern composer."

"Do you think so?" I asked.

"Perhaps."

"And the violin student?"

"Fleur?"

"What a lovely name."

"Yes, rather fanciful. Someone had read Galsworthy. Thank God there are those who have the imagination not to call a child Nancy or Susan. At any rate, Fleur is another protégé of Mr. Saxon's. She's a whizz on her instrument."

"Will she one day be a new Paganini?" I asked, smiling.

"There will never be another Paganini. Or even an Ysaye. But she is very talented."

There was a little silence, during which he looked at me expectantly, and then I realized he was waiting for me to inquire about himself, about his place in the scheme of things at Xanadu.

"And what about you, Mr. ———?" I asked.

44

"Not Mr. Anything," he said. "Just Zoltan. My name is Zoltan Varga, but I am simply Zoltan, if you please. I don't really rate Mister these days. You see, my child, I'm a Schnorrer."

"A *what?*"

He laughed heartily. "You don't know, of course, what that means. Well, it means a cadger, a scrounger, a down-on-his-luck kind of guy." He learned forward. "Let me tell you a story." He cleared his throat. "A Schnorrer is someone who has seen better days. It's a man who has lost his ability to function in a competitive world. The story? Well, there was once a Schnorrer whose daughter fell in love with the son of the richest man in the village. Yes? The rich man was outraged. "My son marry the daughter of a Schnorrer?

"Schnorring is an honorable profession," the Schnorrer said. "Come with me for a day and see how hard one has to work at it.

"The rich man accompanies the Schnorrer from village to village. Finally, at nightfall, the Schnorrer says, 'Now we can go home. We have meat and cheese and quite a bit of cash.' "

" 'Ah, but it's not all that late,' the rich man says. 'We can certainly tackle one more village . . . perhaps two.' "

"So that's what you do," I said, for lack of something better. "You schnorr."

He laughed delightedly. "Yes, I schnorr." Abruptly his face quieted and his eyes were hooded, veiled. Soon, however, he brightened again. "I am an old man. Let someone take care of me. Is there anything wrong with that?"

"I don't think so."

I hadn't the slightest idea what he was driving at.

"You see," he said, "the times pass many of us by. We are on top of things and then . . . pfft . . . we fall to the bottom of the heap. It happens to some of us."

"Yes, I guess so."

The Liszt concerto, in a penultimate tangle of showy chords, built up to its dazzling climax, reached its coda. There was a sudden quiet after it was over.

"Bravo, bravo," Zoltan said softly, and I heard new sounds from the music room, heard Caroline Lance's light, pretty voice and then the deeper one of Alexander Saxon. And then the doors were thrown open and they came out together.

I stood up right away and so, of course, did Zoltan. But it was at Alexander Saxon I looked for my cue as our eyes met: almost imperceptibly he shook his head as if to indicate: *remember you and I are strangers.* He walked toward me. Janet's mother reached me first, however, and took my hands. "Don't tell me this is really little Kip," she said, and my old antipathy toward her came to the fore. The fact was that, irrespective of Janet, Mrs. Lance had always succeeded in bringing out the worst in me. I knew my smile was strained as she trotted over to me on her size five feet, beautifully shod; she was the kind of small, trim woman one instinctively calls 'petite.' Trim of ankle, beautifully preserved, her hair gone white and tinted a glamorous platinum, she looked fifteen years younger than her age. And no wonder, Edward Lance had kept her in cotton batting all her married life, catered to her in every way possible.

She asked me how my dear mother was and said I

was to come visit them at *their* little house very, very soon. Ed would be delighted to see me; when last we met I had been knee-high to a grasshopper. The cliche was uttered with a mischievous smile, as if she had deliberately used it to amuse me. I reflected that, aside from her musical bent, Caroline Lance was a rather stupid woman. She was bright enough, however, to mask her innate dullness with charm, which is, of course, a gift in itself.

She "introduced" me to Alex, who carried off the deception very well, and then Janet came downstairs again.

"The kids are tucked in," she said. "Isn't it nice to see Kip again, Mother?"

"Scrumptious . . . and she's so tall, so pretty."

"And I see you've met Alex," Jan said. "And my friend Zoltan. Now how about . . ."

"Excuse me, everyone, but I must get home," Mrs. Lance said. She took my hands again, gave them a little squeeze and said she'd be seeing a lot of me. I must get out in the sun, too, because I was looking a little bit pale.

I told her there wasn't much opportunity to sunbathe in New York City but that yes, I'd certainly take advantage of the beach here. When she went to the door, with Alex following her, there was the sound of voices and, as Jan's mother left, three other people came in.

Young people. Young and handsome and very with it according to the day's standards. I knew at once, from Zoltan's briefing, that two of them were the young musicians he had told me about. The girl was tall, tanned and fair-haired; the Japanese boy, at least

47

two inches shorter, was appealing, with a shy, slant-eyed smile.

As for the other member of the trio, he was at first only a beautiful blur. For a moment I didn't equate him with gender at all; I was too busy staring, for he had an impact that was almost shattering. His hair, which fell just short of his earlobes, was more silver than gold; he wore very short shorts and his magnificent, lean torso was bare, showing his navel. He was bronzed to the color of mahogany and his long, strong-muscled legs were exquisitely molded.

In short, he was breathtaking to look at. He struck me as either the epitome of purity, all gold and bronze, or as the apotheosis of evil. He was an extravaganza; he looked like Dedealus . . . or Lucifer . . . and a poem of Baudelaire's came to mind: 'O grandest of the angels, and most wise/O fallen god, fate-driven from the skies . . .'

Janet made the introductions.

"Here's Kip," she said. And to me, "Fleur, Tony, Dennis."

The girl held out a long-fingered hand. She had the still unformed body of a child, almost breastless, yet she was very feminine. Tony, grinning, grasped my hand immediately afterwards but Dennis merely put a finger to his forehead. "Pleesameetcha," he said laconically, and when Janet asked him if he could stay to dinner he nodded, didn't say thank you, and then all three of them stampeded upstairs, laughing and knocking against the banister.

"The younger generation," Janet remarked, raising an eyebrow. "Oh, well, we had our turn. Want to see around the house?"

"I'd love to."

We went up; Janet indicated a door. "My room," she said. "Now let's leave your things in yours. I hope you'll like it and will sleep well. Here it is, Kip."

It was a large, square room with a country and sea smell, a big, high bed and a direct view of the ocean from the Moorish balcony. I took to it straightaway and told Janet that I was happy as a clam, that I loved her house and would enjoy every minute of my stay.

"How long can you be with us?" she asked and, for a moment, I wondered if I was to be granted a circumscribed stay, but this rather discomfiting impression was dispelled almost instantly. "You see," she said, "this is something of a bonanza for me. I won't go into any details, Kip, but I'm in kind of a low period at the moment."

She sat down on the edge of the bed and pulled out a cigarette from her purse and held a lighter to it. "Remember chemistry?" she said, looking up at me. "The catalytic agent . . . well, it's funny, but you came at a . . . oh, *particular* time, when I ——"

She broke off and looked out the window onto the narrow balcony and her eyes were very large and unseeing. I remembered that look. That look meant that she was weighing what she was going to say next. And I knew better than to prod. I simply waited for her to finish what she wanted to tell me.

"Can you stay for quite a while?" she asked finally.

"What's quite a while?" I asked.

"A few weeks."

I was surprised. A few weeks? I hadn't anticipated more than a week . . . or at the most two weeks.

"I thought maybe a few days," I said. "A week, perhaps. Or even a bit over that."

"Is that to be all?"

Her face was disappointed: clearly she was let down.

I sat down beside her. "Do you have some kind of emotional deadline?" I asked.

She looked at me for a few seconds and then she smiled. "Well, that's a rather darling way of putting it," she said, and her face cleared. She faced me for a while longer and then she threw back her head and laughed, naturally, in a relaxed way. "You are still the zany, deadpan kid I used to think so much of," she said, and, still laughing, took my face in her hands and gave me a quick kiss on the cheek. *"Doesn't* this bring things back?" she cried. "And weren't those golden days? Norma and I . . . the things we used to be up to! Innocent by today's standards, I realize, and it makes me feel an old fuddy duddy. But for *our* time we were quite something."

She lay back on the bed and looked up at the ceiling. "Norma and I . . . we were considered *very* fast. And I guess we were no better than we should have been. But you didn't know about all that. With you, we were careful to be our best selves. Kip, remember Sunday mornings at Spring Street? When our boy-friends used to come for breakfast and your mother made griddle cakes with Vermont maple syrup? It was so nice. She never said, 'No men in the rooms.' She *trusted* us. It was so much better than if she'd been an old sourpuss."

Jan moved until her head rested in my lap. "And we behaved fairly well," she murmured. "At least I know

50

I never did *really* nefarious things in that room on Spring Street."

"My mother's quite a bright woman," I said, moved. "I guess she figured that her honor system would prevent undesirable results."

"A dear, dear lady," Janet said, and then sat up again. And wonderfully and easily, the first strangeness had passed. We had moved back, a little, in time, and were becoming the way we had used to be. Friends, with memories, perfumed and precious, to bind us together.

She got up and brushed a hand over her hair and said that I must see her studio while it was still light.

She led me up a story, to the top floor. "This is Alex's den," she said, pointing to a partially opened door. "And just down here is where I do *my* work."

Just outside the closed door she paused. The hall was darkening at seven in the evening, and Janet's large eyes swam in front of me. "This is a big, roomy house," she said. "But it's not exactly what I would have chosen. When I think of all those light and airy redwood houses cantilevered over the cliffs . . . like Henry Miller's or Kim Novak's, I could die. But Alex is nothing if not dictatorial. He fell in love with this monstrosity and I'm stuck with it."

"Oh, but it's fabulous," I objected. "It's Edward Hopper, or Charles Addams. You're not really the cantilevered redwood type, Jan."

"I don't know what type I am," she said, shrugging, and smiling faintly as she threw open the door to her workroom. "Come on in," she said. "I know you'll like this. Anyone would. And especially an artist."

It was a breathtaking room. It looked out over the

51

sea and had an uninterrupted view of the sky. It was immense. I gauged it to be about thirty by forty. "This is where I live," Janet said, lightly touching an unfinished painting on an easel. "It's quite wonderful, isn't it?"

"It's . . ." But I was speechless. To work in a room like this . . . why, it was a whole life . . . and that was appreciably what Janet had just said.

"I sometimes spend whole days in here," she told me. "There's a bathroom, the day bed, everything." A satisfied expression stole over her face. "This room is me," she said softly. "Everything else is . . . all of us. But this is me, me. Janet Lance."

I was struck by what she had called herself. Not Janet Saxon, but Janet Lance. I went over the partially-done oil on the easel. It was a littoral landscape, sea and sand and sky, done entirely with a palette knife, without brush work. "Yes, it's a new exploration of mine," she said. "I've dabbled in pointillism, played around with abstractions and was on a primitive kick at one time. Now I'm having fun using only the knife."

"You seem to be trying to simplify," I observed.

"Yes, isn't that more or less what it's all *about*? To purify, refine . . ." She studied the seascape. "I do think I'm getting somewhere," she commented, and then drew her shoulders up, after which she sighed. "What would one do without one's work? Without these saving resources?"

"Yes, I understand that."

She was quiet for a while, looking at the blobs of color on the canvas. Then she straightened up and said, "All right, now you must go to your room and change into something cool and comfy. Then go down to the sundeck. We have our drinks out there. And dinner too."

"All right, Jan."

We went down the one flight to the bedroom areas and she left me. "Any old thing," she said. "We don't dress up like the Englishman in the desert. Just shorts and a shirt. Is there anything you need, Kip?"

"No, I'm sure I have whatever is necessary," I said, and watched her walk down the hall to her own room.

I stripped, changed into pants and a halter after showering, and went on down. It was nice. I heard voices from all over the house; there was the bustle and activity of a complex menage, and I thought it would be pleasant not to live entirely alone.

I went down to the sundeck, a very broad, pleasant adjunct to the back of the house overlooking the sea, with redwood planking made gray by wind and weather. There was nobody there except for a house-hold couple, a man and a woman laying places on a cherry-colored damask cloth-covered round table. They were Orientals and the woman introduced herself and her husband. "I'm Gertrude," she said. "This is my husband, Tom."

"I'm Kip Cornwall."

"May I fix a drink for you?" Tom asked, his crooked teeth flashing in a smile.

"Thanks, but do you think I'd have time to go down and take a look at the beach before the others come down?"

Gertrude bobbed her head. "Sure," she said, consulting a very solid-looking watch on her wrist. "Dinner at nine o'clock, Missy Janet say."

I looked at my own wrist. It was just short of seven-thirty. "Then I'll just go wondering for a short while," I said, and left them to their chores. There was a long flight of wooden steps leading downwards and I made my way, down this rude staircase, to the beach. I was in the thick of verdure of the most lush kind; this was the famed Big Sur, wild and opulent and exotic, an extravagance of nature. It was mountainous terrain that culminated in a breathtaking beach whose coastline seemed to stretch into infinity. I made my way through twisted cypresses and nettles, saw a profusion of scarlet poppies, bushes with white flowers like little stars and others with dark red berries. There was a sprinkling of heavenly blue flowers here and there.

I bent to pick one of the blue flowers.

"Those are lupines," a voice said, and I jumped. It was Dennis, close at my heels.

"Oh, hi," I said, taken aback. I hadn't heard his footsteps.

"Keen, aren't they?"

"Yes, they're lovely," I pointed. "So are those. What are they?"

"Manzanita."

"And that?"

"Scrub oak," he said, following my eyes. "Looks like Christmas holly, yeah?"

"Yes, it does."

He kept on with me as I headed for the beach. It seemed I was to have company on my walk, a self-appointed guide. "This is ice plant," he told me, flicking a bush with pink blossoms. "And this is poison oak. It won't kill you, so don't back off that way."

The poppies grew everywhere, crimson and lush. And as we made our way downwards, an astonishing stand of redwood trees, like somber giants, grew out of the soil like an incredible miracle. I had seen beautiful country before, but I had to admit that this was, by far, the most spectacular.

"You like?" Dennis asked, with a kind of mocking interrogation in his voice.

"Good heavens, yes. This is paradise." And it was. Like the Garden of Eden.

We had by this time reached the lonely sands, an endless stretch with only the chatter of the sandpipers to break the immense silence . . . that and the thundering roll of the breakers. We walked down to the edge of the water. It was wild and beautifully desolate, and there was a high, chilly wind. I gazed my fill and then started plodding across the damp sand.

Dennis walked beside me, on the water side. I didn't really feel like talking because it was all so hypnotic, but I didn't have to say very much. My companion chattered like a magpie.

"So you're a friend of Janet's."

"Yes, I've known her for years."

"Oh?"

"Forever, in fact."

"Forever's a long time."

"You know what I mean. Ever since I was a kid."

"Oh."

Then he said, "You're pretty."

"Thanks," I said, and said it absently. I was busy savoring the ambience, the intense blue of the sky and the breaking surf.

"How come you're a friend of someone Janet's age?"

"She's only ten years older. Or something like that."

"Still, how come?"

"She went to college where I lived, and she roomed with us. My mother and I. And another good friend, a classmate of hers."

"Your mother and you? Don't you have a father?"

"No. He died when I was eight."

"Where do you live?"

"In New York."

"That cruddy place."

"Its all right. My work is there."

"Janet's a good egg," he said unexpectedly.

"I've always thought so."

"What do you do?"

"I'm an artist too. Like Janet."

"Make a living at it?"

"Yes."

"How old are you?"

"Twenty-six. Almost twenty-seven."

"Christ," he said. "You don't look it."

"It's not very old, as a matter of fact. How old are you?"

"Seventeen."

"Do you live around here?"

"Yeah, down the beach aways."

There was a rather welcome silence and then he said, "My mother's an artist too."

"Oh, really?"

56

"Yeah. A good one."

"Marvelous."

"We get along pretty good," he said gruffly.

"I'm glad to hear that," I said. "What about your father? What does he do?"

"He heads a motion picture company. They're divorced."

"Oh, I'm sorry."

"So what? It happens all the time."

"It happens a lot," I agreed.

"But why do people like that have children?"

It threw me, of course. I said carefully, "Because they don't know they're going to . . . to get a divorce, when they get married."

"They ought to know. And they shouldn't have kids."

"Give them a break," I suggested.

"Why?" He stood still, at the water's edge. "Did they give me a break?"

"I'm sure they're both very concerned about you," I said.

"Yeah. Very funny. They're killing themselves, being concerned."

His face darkened. "Ah, screw it." Then he burst out with, "*He* takes a different starlet to dinner every night. You think he wastes time worrying over *me*? *My* parents, you know. Of course he'll open doors. *My* son, the gorgeous junior member of the family. Look how he looks. That hair, those teeth . . ."

He threw back his head and laughed. "They do all these terrific things for you. Great big deal . . ."

It was an old story, one everyone had heard before. What could you say?

Everyone was on the sundeck when we climbed the wooden stairs again. Everyone except Janet. I said I was going upstairs to get the sand from between my toes, but it was really to find my friend. And when I rinsed off my feet and changed my sandals I went down the hall to her room. The door was almost closed but not quite, and I was just about to rap on it when I heard her voice.

I stood outside, heard the sounds drifting up from the sundeck below, and waited. Then I heard Janet again and realized that she was talking on the telephone.

Oh, I thought, and hesitated.

Her voice was brisk, not at all lowered, but there was no reason for her to soft-pedal . . . except that something made me linger there, a sixth sense that warned me.

I didn't know why.

I listened to the familiar vocal sounds, the mid-Eastern "a" which she had not lost, and the quick, decisive way of addressing her listener.

She said, "Im trying to get her to stay on indefinitely."

I drew back. Why, she was talking to someone about *me*.

"Now don't act like a spoiled child," she said. "I want to tell you something, Howard. Her coming here has started me thinking about things, *everything*. She . . . what's that?"

There was a little silence and then she went on. "A danger? What makes you think that?"

This time there was a much longer silence.

And then at last, while I listened shamelessly, she

58

said in a clear, hard voice, "Yes, that could be. Yes, she could conceivably upset the apple cart. Yes, she could start probing. Does that frighten you, Howard?"

I swallowed, shifted carefully, keeping perfectly still, and avidly pressed my ear to the door. A burst of sound issued up from below, so that whatever came next was drowned out. When I could hear Janet again the quality of her voice had changed. It was now quiet, tired, patient. It was . . . as if she had been through these interminable telephone calls time and again.

"Yes," she said. "I do. You know that."

Another silence and then, "That's true. God help me."

She added, rapidly, "I'll see you when I can. What? No, you're to stay where you are. I'll ——"

After one last long silence she said, "All right, Howard. I must go now. Good-bye."

At the click of the receiver being dropped into its cradle I fled. I went quickly down the stairs and then through the lower rooms to the outside area. I was sure I knew whom Janet had been talking to. She had been talking to the fair-haired man I'd seen, first in the restaurant and then in the little waterfront corner of the city called Ghiradelli Square.

And I finally encapsuled Janet's problem, which was nothing very unusual. She *was* having an affair, and that was why her marriage had turned sour.

Oh, poor Alex, I thought and then, *poor Janet.*

Chapter 5

I went outside to the sundeck. Besides the colorfully-laid, huge round table, which now had seven places with china and crystal and silver, there was a drink cart. Tony was standing next to it, openning a bottle of Dr. Pepper.

I was greeted cordially: Zoltan patted a place next to him on a canvas-covered glider and Alex got up right away and asked me what I wanted to drink. I said just scotch and water, please, and he brought it over to me. He gave me a quick, encompassing glance which was warm and friendly and which had just the faintest hint of conspiracy in it.

We were supposed to be strangers, his look seemed to say, but we knew differently, didn't we?

Fleur and Dennis were playing Scrabble, both on their stomachs on the gray, weathered boards of the deck. But after a while they tired of it and pushed the game aside. Dennis rolled over on his back, looking up at the sky, and Fleur came over and sat at my feet.

"You're an artist, like Mrs. Saxon," she said.

"Yes, Fleur."

"I like creative people," she said. "It's wonderful to be living here, with Mr. and Mrs. Saxon, who are both so terrifically talented."

"Hey, what about me?" Tony asked, grinning.

"Yes, you too," Fleur concurred. "And Zoltan, who's always busy at his typewriter. It's like a *kibbutz*. Everyone doing their own thing, and then when we're finished we talk about our achievements . . . or our failures. I do so love it here."

She stretched out her stunning long legs and leaned on an elbow. Her large brown eyes looked up at me. "Are you engaged or anything?" she asked.

"Not yet. That comes later. Right now my work occupies all my time."

"I understand," she said, her chin strong and determined. "Me too. It's the most important thing."

"Ditto," Tony agreed, and raised two fingers in the V sign. "Over the top, mates."

"I got my own ambitions," Dennis muttered, from the floor. "I'll get filthy rich and buy the studio out from under my father. That's *my* goal in life."

"Darling, don't be bitter," Fleur said, but her eyes were soft and kind.

"Good luck to your dreams," Zoltan murmured.

"Oh, I hope we make it, make it big," Tony said, his eyes shining.

Zoltan smiled lazily. "Hope? What an archaic word. Left over from the fifth century. Isn't it rather out of style these days?"

"It will never be out of style," Alex said easily. "It's one of the most important words of all. How else can we live? *These* days, Zoltan? Every era is one of anxiety and fear, disillusionment and heartache. The only salvation is that out-dated word, hope. The affirmation of the future. Without it man would die."

" 'To will the good for the sake of the reward is, as it were, a symbol of double-mindedness.' " Zoltan quoted and turned smilingly to me as he got up to go to the whisky table. "Kierkegaard. A Pollyanna philosopher. I prefer Schopenhauer, the eternal pessimist."

He had a kind of duck walk, his heavy body waddling from side to side as he ambled over to where the liquor supply was. "I am a realist," he admitted. "Neither hope nor affirmation cuts any ice with me. What happens is something to be dealt with in the moment in which it takes you by surprise. Hope? Forget it. If you are well today, so much the better. If sick tomorrow, why it was only to be expected. Hope is just another four-letter word."

"We disagree on friendly terms, I trust," Alex said, smiling, and Zoltan answered, "Like Voltaire, I will defend to the death the right to your opinions, which are totally diametric to mine." His smile was genial. "That's what makes horse races, or so they say."

And then Janet walked out to join us, lifting a hand in greeting. She had changed into jeans and a yellow shirt that flapped loosely, and had unbound her hair so that it feel carelessly over her shoulders.

Suddenly she was the girl of yesterday, hauntingly young, as if time had not only come to a stop but had moved backwards, and I saw her, thrillingly, as she used to be, making her way across the campus, books under her arms and those long, swinging legs . . .

She sat down between me and Zoltan on the glider

and Alex got up to make her the drink she asked for. And as if it were a signal, the group suddenly took on life and meaning, with Janet there with us.

She raised her glass. "Cheero," she said, and her lips were soft and smiling. She leaned against me and added, "Lord, it's good to have you here, darling. Isn't it nice to have Kip, you guys? It's funny what suddenly comes to my mind. I don't know what made me think of this."

She took a sip of her drink and slid down in her seat, quoting.

" 'Full merrily the bumble-bee doth sing/Till he hath lost his honey and his sting/And being once subdued in armed tail/Sweet honey and sweet notes together fail . . .' "

"What is that?" Fleur asked, looking up.

"Ask Zoltan," Janet said.

"Zoltan?"

"Shakespeare," he said.

"You see? Zoltan knows."

"How'd you know that?" Tony demanded, impressed.

"Because I know literature. I can't earn a living, but that's beside the point at the moment."

"Zoltan is one of a vanishing breed," Janet said. "We don't care about our intellectuals any more."

She had her head back against the glider, and her long hair, with its streak of white at the temple, tangled in the web of the wrought iron. She was so beautiful, so charismatic. I couldn't keep my eyes off her.

I had often thought that being with Janet was like being at a party, but what I had meant by that was something very different from the way it might sound.

64

Because Janet had always been a quiet, private person; yet when you were with her you relaxed and enjoyed . . . and you were the one who laughed and became alive, because she brought you out of yourself, was the touchstone that made you breathe wide and free.

We sat, talking and gossiping and drinking, while the evening waned and the bright, sunlit afternoon turned to dusk. There was laughter and cheer and friendship, and when we pulled up our chairs at the great round table we were, I decided, like old friends. There was a Japanese dish, which Janet told me was called Kyoto, a delicious casserole with chicken, meat patties, artichoke hearts and prawns, done to a succulent turn.

"Yes, Gertrude's a superb cook," Alex said when I praised the meal. "We dine well."

"I should say so. Everything was sublime."

We had brandies; the light was violet. Only the candles lit the purple dusk. Zoltan, who was clearly a favorite of Janet's, was telling us about his first literary effort.

"A small, silly little play I dreamed up," he said. "I was nineteen years old and someone got me an audience with Artur Schnitzler. He read my play and said it was quite good."

"Was it a success?" Fleur asked.

"Certainly not. It never saw the light of day."

He looked round, flushed with food and brandy. "Yet how many have received encouraging words from the most illustrious of Viennese playwrights? It gave me confidence. And then, only a year later, I met Ferenc Molnar."

"Who's that?" Fleur asked innocently.

"Molnar? You don't know who he is? He made a fortune, and a great name, in his lifetime."

There was a silence.

"Molnar," Zoltan said, "was the greatest commercial dramatist to emerge from Hungary. His best known work is *Liliom,* which two gentlemen, named Rogers and Hammerstein, turned into a show called *Carousel.*"

"Oh, shoot, *that,*" Tony cried. "Everyone knows *Carousel.* Kitschy, but pretty good just the same."

"That's fame for you," Zoltan said dryly. "Rogers and Hammerstein. The hell with poor old Molnar. Oh well, it happens to all of us. The times pass us by."

"Never mind," Janet said. "Youth will be served, we all know that." She turned to me, and in the light of the candles her eyes were gleaming, lustrous. It was dark now, really dark. Except for the candles. "Kip, he's teaching me Hungarian. How do you like that?"

"Oh, he is?"

She laughed. "It wouldn't get me very far in Budapest, and according to Zoltan my accent's deplorable. But still . . ."

"Go ahead," Zoltan urged. "Show off a little."

"Okay. I can say thank you. *Koszonom Szepen.*"

"Very good," Zoltan praised.

"Very good? *Nagyon Jo.*"

"What else?" Tony asked, leaning his elbows on the table.

"Oh . . . let's see. Good-bye. *A Viszontlatasra.* How's that?"

There was general handclapping. "Bravo," Tony said, leading the claque.

"I've learned plenty from Zoltan." Janet said. "For example, Kip, did you know that history was made in bed?"

"*What?*"

"According to Zoltan—and I trust him implicitly—it *was*. That is to say, the mistresses of great men shaped history in their boudoirs. Madame Pompadour, La Valliere, Josephine Beauharnais . . . it was the women who made things happen the way they did."

"And Draga Masin?" I asked.

At once Zoltan was in a transport. "Listen to her," he cried. "She knows the Austro-Hungarian history! Draga Mashin . . . why, you're a young wonder, my pretty child."

And when the others, Fleur and Tony and Dennis, asked what he was talking about, he told them the bloody story of the Serbo-Croatian prostitute who captured the fancy of King Alexander, who married her and made her Queen of the Empire. And about how she had died on her battlefield, the bed, raped by the vassals of Peter Karageorgeovitch and then pierced through by a dagger.

"The murder took place in another courtesan's bed," Alex said, when my moment of glory had died down.

Zoltan's eyes sharpened. "So. We have two students of history here," he said. "Yes? Alex is right. Queen Draga Mashin met her gory end in the bed of one of the most famous mistresses of all time. But Mr. Saxon will explain."

"What?" Tony asked eagerly. "What does Zoltan mean?"

Alex smiled. "Why, the bed the royal couple slept in was a wedding gift from the French government to Alexander and Draga."

"Yes?"

"It had belonged to Madame Dubarry in her lifetime."

"But that's fascinating," Fleur said. "How do you know all this?"

"There are other things in life besides music," Alex said.

It was good conversation, and a kind of lesson to the arrogant young and I was glad for it. The candles flickered and the roar of the surf crashed over the rocks down below. Suddenly New York, and the Upper East Side, seemed not only very far away in miles but also in meaning. As if I had landed on another planet.

The sky overhead was specked with stars. Millions of them, trillions. I shivered. It was such a vast universe.

Later, we went for a walk on the beach, Alex, Janet and I. "It'll be coolish," Janet warned me. "Better put on a cardigan."

"All right, I'll go and get one."

"Never mind, use one of mine," she said carelessly, and led me into her bedroom, which was very much like mine except that I could see that it had an adjacent dressing room. Jan fished out a couple of sweaters from a closet with louvred doors, threw me one and shrugged into the other, then as we left her bedroom, switched out the overhead light, leaving a couple of lamps burning. When we closed the door and stood in the hall another door opened down the hall and

Janet's husband came out. The light was on and Alex was framed, for an instant, in the doorway.

Something clicked . . . something adjusted in my mind. Janet . . . Janet's bedroom. And down the hall Alex, and Alex's bedroom. I knew, instantly and with a flash of comprehension, that this separate bedroom business was of long standing. Why? Because neither of them was self-conscious about it. They had forgotten about anything else; neither of them considered it any more.

I did some rapid mental calculation. Roger, the younger Saxon child, was four years old. That might very well mean that for four years these two married people had been living separately under one roof.

It didn't necessarily mean that . . . or anything, I told myself. And yet I knew it could mean everything.

In the dark we made our way, down the rustic steps, to the beach.

We walked along the edge of the sea, scarcely saying a word, for perhaps three quarters of an hour. Then Janet guessed we had gone far enough. "I'm falling asleep on my feet," she said.

"I suppose Katherine must be tired as well," Alex answered.

"You call her Katherine," Janet said, her voice coming out of the darkness. "Why?"

There was a charged silence. I thought, how awkward, how awkward . . . There was no way Alex could know my name was Katherine, unless Janet had told him so, and clearly, she hadn't. Kip, of course, could mean anything.

"I didn't think it was short for Kipling, as in Rudyard," Alex said imperturbably. "What else could it be but Katherine? Correct me if I'm wrong."

"No, you're right," I said quickly. "It's Katherine. Kip's a holdover from my tender years. I suppose I should be grateful it wasn't Kitty."

In my room I got ready for bed. It had been a long day and, although there were some questions in my mind, they were tabled. The afternoon and evening had been so wonderful, so exciting and filled with friendship and laughter, that everything else was pushed to the side. I was thinking of the drinks and dinner on the sundeck, with the beautiful young people, sublime in their ignorance and youth, and of Alex, smiling quietly, of Janet, radiant, and Zoltan, the compleat intellectual.

I was thinking of the darkening sky after the resplendence of the sunset, and the roar of the surf from down below. The candles in the dark, the starry sky. And then the black night and the cool sand under our feet as we walked along shore.

I was keyed up, of course, wondering whether I could sleep. My body was tired but my mind was hyperactive. After all those years . . . to see Janet again, wife, mother and doyenne of a household. It was just after midnight when I got into my nightgown. I fiddled around for a while, and then made up my mind. I would go down the hall and say a last goodnight to Janet. Just say, "Night night, darling, I'll see you in the morning."

And then she would say, with a kiss on my cheek, "Sleep well, darling." I was sure she would. She had said it so many times, years ago. "Close your eyes, Kip . . . go to sleep, baby."

70

I stood there hesitating and then I put a robe over my nightie and opened my door. All was silent. With an expectant smile on my face I walked quietly down the hall to Jan's door, at the end of the hall and on the sea side, like my own. I almost knocked . . . I heard something, and my hand fell down to my side.

I heard someone crying.

I stood there, wondering if I could be mistaken. I looked about quickly . . . but the hall was empty. So I leaned closer to the door. There . . . there it was again . . .

A dry sob, unmistakable, reached me. Not loud, but muffled, as if into a pillow.

She's crying, I thought. Janet was crying . . . all alone, in her separate bedroom.

Across the hall, down a little way, a rim of light shone under Alexander Saxon's door. He doesn't hear Janet weeping, I thought . . . or he doesn't want to hear.

I forced myself to leave that closed door, to go away from the inexplicable grief that lay just inside it. I had to. Jan was a married woman, a mother, with a husband almost across the corridor from her. How could I presume to intrude on her sorrows . . . whatever they were?

Why? I wondered, back in my room. Why should Janet be unhappy? With seemingly so much?

"I love my wife," Alexander Saxon had said. And I had believed him.

Did I still believe him?

Troubled, I drifted off to sleep. I don't think I dreamed. If I did, it made no impression. Because, when I woke, nothing lingered. I simply opened my eyes and I knew someone was in my room.

There was bright moonlight.

I heard the sound and then I lay stiffly, alerted. The sound was breathing, and it was very close to me.

Breathing . . . almost in my ear.

I tensed.

There's someone here, I thought. Who?

A shadow bent over me and suddenly I was no longer inert. I gasped, moved, and a scream, ready to burst forth, gathered momentum inside me. A hand came over my mouth and clamped off the scream, still unborn.

"It's all right, Kip."

I knew the voice instantly, and subsided. Surprised? Of course. I sat up.

"It's only me," Janet's voice said.

"Janet . . ."

"I'm sorry."

"What is it?"

"Nothing. I just wanted to . . . to see if you needed anything."

Wonderingly, I looked at her. Her face, in the silvery moonlight, was vague, only half defined. "I don't need anything," I said, and it sounded so incredible, so foolish, that I almost laughed. That I would be needing anything in the middle of the night.

"You must forgive me," she said quickly. "I didn't mean to wake you up. Sometimes . . . sometimes I can't sleep, you see. And I suppose I wanted to make sure you were really here, that it wasn't a dream. Oh, Kip, all sorts of things are coming back to me. That house on Spring Street with you and me and Norma and the others. Your mother. I was so young. I try to assure myself that I was once that young. It was so wonderful and safe and . . ."

She broke off.

I felt her get up, and reached out.

"No, don't go," I said. "Not yet. Let's have a cigarette. Don't go yet, Janet."

"All right," she said.

I got out of bed and fished for my pack. Then I lit one and gave it to Janet. After that I lit my own. We sat there, on the edge of the bed, an ashtray balanced between us, in the moonlit darkness, and talked. About the old days, about the good and bad roommates in my mother's house, and about the campus, in all the seasons. Spring, with the blossoms, and then the green summer. Fall, with the leaves turning russet and golden . . . and winter, all snow and ice and frozen beauty.

"I'd forgotten," Janet said. "Imagine . . . I'd forgotten."

"Not me," I said.

"You were fond of us, weren't you? Norma and me."

"You were my life."

Her voice was soft. "Imagine that."

"I used to think . . . oh, that I wanted to do something wonderful for you. I pictured you drowning, and that I'd save you." The darkness covered my confusion, the revelation of those youthful dreams. "I thought if I could do something gallant. . ."

"That's very sweet," she said. "But I didn't need help then."

"Do you now?" I asked.

There was a long, very long silence. Then, "But if I

did, what could you possibly do?" she asked, with a strange note in her voice.

"Something," I said. "I'd do something."

"Would you, now?"

"Yes, Janet. Yes."

And then she got up. "All right, Kip, I've disturbed your sleep. You must linger in bed very late. Forgive me, I shouldn't have come in like this."

"I'm glad you did. I was feeling a little lost."

"Were you?"

"Because, you see, it was all so long ago for me too."

I felt her hand on my face. "I'm so glad you're here," she said. "Everything, somehow, looks a little different now. I needed a transfusion . . . you're it, Kip."

Her mouth brushed my cheek lightly. And then she glided out, her nightgown a froth around her, her tall, lean body outlined in the doorway. She stepped outside into the hall, and the door closed.

I fell asleep but not for long. As if someone had pressed a button to release a hidden spring in my mind, I woke suddenly and turned over on my back.

"But I didn't need help then . . ."

Why, she had thrown me a cue!

And then other things. The conversation with that man . . . Howard . . . *"Yes, she may upset the apple cart . . ."*

A little thrill ran through me. It was not at all pleasant. On the contrary, it was quite cold and wary, as if now I had been warned. Of course in the middle of the night, one's imagination is heightened, perceptions are sharpened and the voice of doom speaks louder than

74

at any other time. But I felt very odd, as if . . . well, as if Janet meant to use me, to take advantage of my presence on the premises to —

To do what?

Did the fair princess wish St. George to slay the dragon?

I had offered, substantially, to be St. George. Hadn't I?

I turned over, impatient with myself and faintly headachy. The surf thundered down below and for the first time I wished it would stop. I found myself counting, out of a desire to quell my thoughts and get back to sleep again.

One, two, three . . . crash.

And then one, two, three . . . the sigh of the waters drawing back.

And then again . . . crash.

Oh, for Christ's sake, I thought . . . drop the other shoe. I burrowed into my pillow with my eyes screwed shut. And of course I finally fell asleep. You always did, sooner or later.

Chapter 6

I slept lightly and at six o'clock, unable to stay in bed any longer, got up and opened my door. The house was silent. I had promised to call Norma as soon as possible, and besides, I could scarcely wait to. In the east it would be nine o'clock; Norma would be up, fixing breakfast for her husband, steaming bottles for the baby. I went downstairs, blinking in the early morning sunlight, to the living room that was on the other side of the entrance hall from the music room. There was a phone on a pickled pine desk and I put through a person to person call, collect.

"I'm so relieved to hear from you," Norma said when she answered. "How's Jan?"

"Sort of changed," I said.

"Tell me."

I did, trying to be brief. I felt like a thief in the wee hours of the morning, stealing downstairs secretly, "reporting" on a friend. "She's distressed in some way," I said.

"What do you mean?"

"Oh . . . a few nebulous things that might not amount to very much, but . . . well, for example, she was crying last night when I went to see her just before bed."

"Speak louder," Norma said. "I can't hear you properly. You say she was crying? Did they have a fight?"

"No. But they don't sleep together. That is, they have separate bedrooms."

"Please, Kip, speak into the phone. I can't *hear* you."

"I *can't* talk louder. Someone might hear me."

But after all I was all alone: the rest of them were sleeping. I said, "Norma, I just don't want to be over-heard. But I suppose it's all right. It's only six o'clock here. Well then, about Janet. They have separate bed-rooms. I was . . . surprised."

"That doesn't mean anything," Norma said. "But she was crying, right?"

"Yes, and in San Francisco she flared up at a police-man." I felt helpless and ineffectual. It all sounded so insane. A tiff with a traffic cop, separate rooms, women, and men too, cried in the night. What did it all add up to?

"She may be having an affair," I said, and knew that I was intent on shocking Norma into an involve-ment with *my* involvement. "She was having drinks with a man at the Fairmont Hotel. I stumbled into it accidentally. She didn't see me."

"Oh, dear," Norma said. "Oh, Kip, I'm sorry to hear that."

"Yet I can't believe it of Janet," I said quickly. "I

just can't think it's as simple as that. There's a house in San Francisco. I saw him go in there."

"Him? You mean Janet's lover?"

I hated the sound of that. Again I thought of Alexander Saxon and how much I admired and liked him. I said, suddenly perverse, or just plain stubborn, "I didn't say she had a lover. I said——"

"If she's having an affair, then she has a lover," Norma pointed out, and I knew that the sharpness of her voice was because she felt the same way I did . . . sad, irritable and unhappy. "There's some man, that's true, but I——"

I broke off. "I know where he lives," I went on. "I know his name . . . that is to say, his first name. Howard. I'm going to try to find out something about him. I don't know. I just don't know. I have this odd feeling that there's more to this than meets the eye. Janet's acting strangely . . . most unpredictably."

"But what else could it mean?"

"I'll find out," I said. "Somehow. There's something going on here, something I can't understand yet, but I won't leave here until I get to the bottom of it."

I hadn't intended any such thing. Furthermore I hadn't, in my conscious mind, been convinced that there was "something going on here." Yet apparently, in my deepest subconscious, undefined but urgent, there was a strong sense of a gigantic problem in Janet's life, that it wasn't only that she was having an affair.

"I wish I could help," Norma said. "If you can't always make a call, write me." I heard the sudden wail of an infant in the background. She was busy . . . there was no one to help Janet but me.

79

"I'll see what I can get out of Jan's mother," I said quickly.

"Her *mother*?"

"They're living here, believe it or not. Yes, just around the corner. You see how things are? Yes, Norma, I'll write if I can't call you. I have nothing to go on. Keep well, and much love."

"Well, I'm terribly upset," she said fretfully.

"Yeah, me too."

"Keep in touch. Mind, now. I want to know what's going on."

"Yes, Norma, one way or the other. Either the phone, or a letter."

"Then good-bye, for now anyway, Kip."

I was putting the receiver back in its cradle when I heard it. A distinct click. I went a little cold. I could have been mistaken. It sounded, though, like a third party hanging up.

But I could have been mistaken . . . ?

Just the same, I was chilled. How ghastly! It would be bad enough if Alex had been listening in. But supposing it had been Janet . . . ?

How horrible that would be! To hear those things said about her, in kindness, concern and compassion, but just the same voiced, communicated.

Please, if there was someone listening in, I prayed, let it not have been Janet. It would be so destructive, so traumatic. What a traitor she would think me.

I had imagined everyone still asleep. And yet, and yet . . .

If my ears were to be trusted, someone had put down a receiver just before I had.

And the bad connection . . . Norma saying she couldn't hear me properly . . .

I got up out of my chair, shivering. But it wasn't just because of my apprehensions, I saw. When I had come into the room the windows had been tightly closed. I remembered Jan's saying that, regardless of whatever heat there was during the day, the nights were cool, sometimes uncomfortably so. But now there was a window open. The curtains were blowing inwards, billowing like a sail and whipping sharply against the frame. I hadn't heard anything at all. But it was plain to see that, while I had been talking, someone had opened this window, perhaps entered, and then left without a sound.

My hackles rose: I could feel the hair on my head stiffen. *Without a sound?* the curtains floated like ghostly cerements in the stiff morning breeze. I moved over to the window and looked out. The far vista of the Pacific glistened, but the foliage, trees and rocks shortened a near view. And then I had a quick glimpse of very fair hair, like silver in the sunlight. A shape was revealed, in an aperture between two spiny trees, for a brief moment. Then it disappeared, swallowed up by the sheltering leaves.

That bright head?

Dennis, of course. Of course.

I was angry and distrubed. He seemed to come and go as he pleased. He had heard at least part of what I'd said, perhaps all of it. So that not only had someone been a party to my call on another extension but Dennis, too, had been a witness.

There would be no more telephone calls, I told myself grimly, as I crept upstairs again. I got into bed mostly to keep warm, and it wasn't only the early cool. Had I really heard a click? And had that really been Dennis running down the path?

Or was I hypersensitive . . . imagining things?

I wasn't sure . . . about anything.

And shortly afterwards, I fell into a deep, exhausted sleep.

It was the music that woke me.

As I turned over, with heavy eyes, I thought an orchestra was tuning up, that I was in Carnegie Hall and the musicians were keying their instruments. Then I came back to earth and remembered where I was.

It was a violin, playing the Beethoven D major concerto. Imagine waking to *that*, I told myself, and lay quietly, my ears attuned. The beautiful cadences drifted up from the regions below.

The handle of my door turned slowly. I hastily covered myself with the bedclothes and called out, "Who's there?"

The door opened. "Kip?" a treble voice said. "Are you awake?"

It was Janet's two little boys.

"Come on in," I called out. "Don't be afraid, I won't eat you."

That brought forth a cascade of giggles, and then they walked in, announcing that everyone was up and about except for myself.

"Am I too late for breakfast?"

"No, not *at all*," Alex Junior said, shocked. "You're to eat, Mama said, because you're too thin."

"Did she say that?"

"Yes, and you *are* spindley, Kip."

"I thought of myself as willowy," I objected.

"Just the same you must eat well," he said sternly. "You can have a tray if you want."

"I'd rather go down. Is it all right?"

"Sure, Gertrude will feed you. She's waiting. She sent us up."

"I could be ready in about fifteen minutes."

"You won't take all day, like Fleur?"

"Does Fleur take all day?"

"She does when she and Dennis go out somewhere in the evening."

Roger said, "Do you know Dennis? He's a hippie."

"Yes, I've met him."

"Isn't he beautiful? He looks like Jesus."

"I like Dennis," Alex Junior said.

"I like Dennis too. I like everybody," Roger said magnanimously.

"Do you like me?"

"Yes, you're very pretty," Alex said. "Mama's going to paint you."

"Okay, boys, run along now. I'll shower and dress, and see you in fifteen minutes."

"Very well," Alex said, and grasped his brother's hand. "We must go, you see, because she has to get dressed."

When I went down I heard raised voices from the music room. Before that there was the busy hum of an active household, and it was so nice. There was the click click of a typewriter in Zoltan's room, the sound of a metronome from where Tony was housed . . . and I knew that, on that upper story, Janet was already wielding her brush or palette knife.

But in the music room there was friction. I heard Mendelssohn being played, but in the midst of a passage there was a break and then Alex's voice, impatient and admonitory.

"Uh, uh," he said, and I could picture a frown on his handsome face. "Your tempo, Fleur. This is the third time."

"I'm trying." I heard her say.

"Try harder."

"Oh."

Her voice sounded distressed, and then the music resumed again.

I listened, and found myself tensing up when Fleur came to the crucial passage. And the poor girl, she muffed it once more. Her timing was off. The error was repeated; there was the sound of something being thrown down, perhaps a baton, with a sharp crack. Then the door was flung open and Fleur streaked out, her face flushed and tears brimming in her eyes. I stepped back quickly, but she collided with me, gave me a blind look and rushed on. She threw open the front door and dashed out.

Alex came slowly out of the music room.

"Where did she go?" he asked me.

"Out the front," I said.

"Oh well, I can't blame her. She's rather be playing tennis. These *wunderkind* have a tough time of it." He looked toward the door and then back to me, seeming really to see me for the first time. "Well, good morning," he said. "You've had breakfast?"

"Not yet. Your children woke me up and said I had better get right down. So here I am."

"But that's ridiculous. You could have had it sent up."

"I didn't want that. Thanks just the same."

"The boys haven't been bothering you, have they?"

"Certainly not. They're very well-behaved. But you must excuse me, because they're waiting for me."

"Any reason why I can't join you for a cup of coffee?"

"None at all."

"Then let's go."

Breakfast was served out on the sundeck, which seemed to be the heart and core of the household. "Kip," Alex Junior said, scrambling up from an over-sized lounge chair. "You're right on time," he told me, consulting a Mickey Mouse wristwatch. "I hope you like bacon and eggs, because that's what we told Gertrude to make you."

"Sounds yummy," I said, and all four of us gathered at the round table, laid this morning with a daisy-printed cloth. The boys chattered and it was a jolly breakfast. Afterwards, the children went off to make their beds, since this was a rule of the house, and I was left alone with my host. We made small talk for a while and then he said, "About Janet. How do you find her?"

"Why . . ." I felt awkward, hesitant.

"Do you think she looks well?"

"I think she looks beautiful," I said sincerely.

He frowned. "She *is* beautiful. I didn't mean that."

"Well . . ."

He waited.

"It's just that—"

85

"Yes?"

"I . . ." It was difficult to say these things. Reluctantly, I added, "She doesn't seem completely herself."

"No," he agreed, soberly. "She doesn't. Can you tell me why?"

"No, how can I?"

He looked for a long time at me, and then said, "Have you taken a dislike to me?"

I was totally disconcerted. "Certainly not," I said at last. "What makes you say such a thing?"

"Because—"

"Alex," I said, after a long silence, "I agree that Janet seems to be troubled . . . about something . . . but I have no idea why she is. I'm sorry, that's all I can say at the moment."

Again the long, reflective stare. Then he said, "Okay, shall we let it go? Because I have no wish to distress you."

"It isn't that!" I was vastly uncomfortable. To discuss Janet, even with her husband, seemed so *disloyal*. I was agitated, and my voice rose.

"It's been so many years," I said rebelliously. "I don't really know Janet any more. Can't you see?"

His answer came almost instantly.

"I don't really know her any more either."

It was said almost casually, but his eyes were so somber and bleak that I had to look quickly away. Oh, I thought. What a terrible admission for a husband to make.

But what could I do? Tell him that his wife was almost certainly in love with another man? I felt a brief hostility toward Janet. Wouldn't it be better to be honest? Tell the truth . . . get a divorce . . .

It was always, naturally, for the sake of the children that these faltering marriages were preserved. Yet sooner or later children sensed things. Was there more of a trauma in a clean break than in a home filled with undercurrents which almost always transmitted themselves to those very children who were supposed to be protected . . . at such great cost?

Or was I completely mistaken? Was there some other explanation for Janet's behavior? Did that man have a hold on her other than a sexual one?

"Let's go for a walk," Alex said abruptly.

"Oh . . . yes, fine."

We went down the steep flight of steps, single file, walked leisurely through the sun-dappled foliage and at last reached the silvery sand. "You certainly have privacy," I said. There wasn't a soul around, and if there were houses, they were concealed by the nature of the woody terrain. It was like being entirely alone in a totally unpeopled spot.

"Oh, it's lonely enough," Alex said. "And that's what I prize. I don't care to be cramped . . . or pressed upon. I like to feel space . . ." He looked around. "This is, yes, a compound of far-flung houses. You'll have the beach to yourself. But I must warn you that these waters are dangerous. Don't swim far out, but keep close to the shore. That's an order. You could be swept away in a second. Oh, yes. The cruel sea can be very cruel indeed."

I said I would be very careful. "I'm quite serious," he said, for good measure. "You don't take chances with this surf. So please remember that. And I hope you'll feel at home here. I'm afraid our household is geared to steady and hard work, and I would so regret it if you felt neglected. Janet and I had a talk about it, because she wants you to feel at home. Go wherever you want. There are all those cars, and there's plenty to see around here. Just—

"Just *vacation,*" he said with a smile. "We both know you work hard, so will you be comfortable and at ease and enjoy yourself?"

"Yes," I said. "And thank you. I do work hard, and this is gorgeous country. Please don't try to entertain me, I don't want that. I love this mad dedication to the arts. I *love* it. When I first moved to Manhattan from Massachusetts, I found a little walk-up on Sixth Avenue . . . the Avenue of the Americas, if you will. It was near Carnegie Hall. Every week-end morning I walked the streets and heard the sound of music from studios. Violins and pianos, cellos. Sopranos, good and bad. This reminds me of those pleasant days there."

"Why did you leave that walk-up?" he asked.

"I had no choice. They tore the building down. There's a high-rise now, with rents just as steep."

"It's changed, hasn't it?"

"New York? Vastly. I become ambivalent about it, like everyone else."

"Yes, things do change," he agreed. "Things . . . and people. But only a fool expects life to go on forever in the same way." Another smile, and we walked on, the sand spraying our feet.

"Who's Zoltan?" I asked after a while.

"Oh, just an unfortunate." He shook his head. "Oh, no, that's just the sort of thing *not* to say about Zoltan. He deserves a better epithet than that. He's down on his luck, it's true, but that's not his fault. He got old, and circumstances played against him. He's Hungarian, as you know by now."

Alex laughed. "He likes to talk, doesn't he? And he talks well. He's a conversationalist of the old school. Everything has to be in sentences and paragraphs. I have a feeling that he wakes up in the morning framing dialogue. He's a kind of windbag, admittedly, and often he bores the pants off me. But he's an interesting man, all the same. It's simply that he has no market value."

"What's he doing here?"

"Trying to write. He was once a journalist in Europe, and evidently a highly-paid one. And then in 1958—the great Hungarian revolt, that abortive and tragic quasi-revolution, broke out and Zoltan became a political prisoner, since he was patently to the left. Somehow or other he was finally released and he hotfooted it over here. A friend vouched for him and he got in on a quota."

"Oh, the poor old soul."

"He wasn't exactly received with open arms . . . professionally, that is. He had a series of menial jobs. Janet was the one to meet him, and I know she made many telephone calls, but had little luck. So I . . . well, we love to have him here. I was instantly struck by his courage and his way of rising above the hopelessness of his situation. There are thousands like him; we all know that. If you can help only one of them. It's something, at any rate."

"Yes, it's something indeed. I think it's wonderful of you both. Tell me about the others. Fleur and Tony."

"Well, let's see. Tony's seventeen and his family lives in San Francisco. Lots of kids running about, too many. The mother and father run one of those junky shops with everything in it but the kitchen sink. They barely eke out a living. Tony's the gifted one. The other children are only average. I came across him at the San Francisco Conservatory of Music; it was one of those fortuitous things. He'd gotten a scholarship. I recognized his great talent and so I've taken him on. His parents are piteously grateful. I'm very fond of Tony. He'll go far, I know it."

"And Fleur?"

"She's still just a child, and so enormously malleable. She's just thirteen, you know."

"Is that all? I would have said she was older. Fifteen or sixteen."

"Yes, she's quite the young lady, isn't she? Hers is a rather sad story. She's an orphan, but somehow or other she came to my attention through a musical acquaintance of mine, a violinist. He told me about her, said she was gifted and suggested I hear her. I did. She performed for me and I knew at once that she had rare qualities. I'll give her, as I'll give Tony, as much as I can, then send them both abroad for foreign study. I feel I have two winners, and that's very exciting, you know."

"You must be very pleased."

"I am. Isn't she lovely? Isn't she a beautiful creature?"

I looked up quickly. His voice was enthusiastic, vibrant. And I had the strangest feeling. Fleur was only a child, granted. But she looked older, in spite of her twiggy figure. She seemed more like sixteen, almost, in fact, a woman.

Yet she was only a little girl.

I had the most unpleasant reaction. Alex's voice echoed in my ears. *Isn't she lovely* . . .

Could he possibly be attracted to Fleur? A not yet nubile maiden and yet so talented. He would find that irresistible. She was truly wonderful looking, with her bright, chrysanthemum head, her huge brown eyes.

"Yes, she is lovely," I said.

"That face . . ."

I thought of Fleur's face. Delicate, satin-skinned, heart-shaped. I thought of her tall, child-like body, her long, slender legs. It would be hard for a man, any man, not to see the beauty of that child.

"Look," he said suddenly. "What more can anyone ask?"

We were standing now at a point where the coastline serpentined; there was to our right a rude fence constructed where a kind of dangerous gully sank into the sandy ground. To our left was a tangle of driftwood, as white and silver as the bleached bones of animals, dinosaurs, perhaps. Ahead lay twisted cypresses, leaning so far toward the ground that it seemed as if a breath would loose their decayed roots and send them hurtling to the sand. Several small necks of land were inundated with frothing water and farther out the sea found its way into a rocky cove, splashing and jettying and fountaining sea water into the limpid air. A single, dead tree stump, bent with the inexorable forces of the year-round wind, was white and hollowed and druidical-looking.

"Isn't that nice," Alex said, breathing deeply. "Christ almighty, as if that doesn't make up for everything."

I stood with him and let the sea gales blow over me. Yes, it was beauty incarnate, burning into my soul, into my mind. I thought of the neat, tree-lined Manhattan streets of the east side, the boutiques, the well-kept apartment houses and the co-ops with their four-season's planting. I thought of the posh restaurants and the art-film movie houses, the gala evenings at Lincoln Center, the Ginger Man and the Bethesda Fountain in Central Park, the children's zoo, the art galleries on Madison Avenue, the orderly elegance of Fifty-seventh Street, the funny little, fast-disappearing stores on Second Avenue and First.

That was my life. And shortly, I would go back to it.

We started walking back. "I'm a New Englander born and bred," Alex said reflectively. "I was used to the trim, green box hedges of Salem and Ashfield. Tidy and green and snug. Yes. But I found myself here. Look what I have. This wild, rockbound coast, calling to me, calling to me. Every day, beauty and excitement and wonder. It released me. It opened me up."

I stumbled over a piece of driftwood and he caught me before I fell. "Easy," he said. "All right now?"

"Yes."

"Well, I've been talking like an idiot." He laughed. "And I criticize Zoltan for expounding. It's your fault," he said. "I don't have many people to talk to these days."

I saw that he realized at once his own error, was shamed at it. What he had said was, in effect, I'm lonely, even though with a wife and family . . . and you're a good listener.

And he turned away quickly.

When he looked back at me he started talking again and it was off the top of his head, I thought. Just random talk, which eventually led back to his work again, and his young charges, Tony and Fleur.

"Tony's very smart," he said. "He has a mathematical brain and a poet's heart."

"Yes, he's very endearing. Yes, I do like him."

"And Fleur?"

"She's lovely."

I echoed his former words, and tightened up. Fleur again, I thought. He was simply leading the conversation back to Fleur.

His toes dug into the sand as he walked. Big, strong feet, the feet of my friend's husband. He was splitting a blade of grass. His hair blew back in the wind. Soft hair, thick, but soft.

"Yes, lovely," he said.

He handed me a cattail to behead, as he had been doing. I made a loop in the stem of the cattail, drew it toward the top, and popped the head off. It was a nihilistic act. I only copied what he was doing, but I wondered if, in doing it, Alex was releasing hostility . . . toward someone?

"You'll stay for a while?" he asked.

"Why, I don't intend to wear out my welcome."

"You won't. I hope you'll be here for a good long time. I mean it, you know." He frowned. "I don't know, I don't know," he murmured. "I can't seem to pin down why I'm so concerned about all our lives."

I couldn't think of one single thing to say, and so was silent.

The water foamed up at our feet. The sky, sun-glazed, warmed our shoulders. Alex bent and picked up a small, irridescent shell.

He held the shell in his hands.

"We were once very happy," he said. "At least I thought so. At least I was."

Chapter 7

When we got back to the house Alex excused himself; the violin, faint but filtering back to the sundeck, was audible from the house. "The crisis has passed, thanks be to God," Alex said with a relieved smile, and left me.

I lay down in a beach chair and turned my face up to the sun. I thought, I should go up and change into a bikini, but I was too lazy. It was more than that, of course. It was coming face to face with Janet this morning. I was sure now that Alex hadn't been listening on my call to Norma: if he had, there would surely have been a comment.

Then had it been Janet?

I was very uneasy. There were magazines in an iron rack; I pulled a couple out, but the sun put me to sleep and I could feel them sliding out of my hands and I didn't care. I could feel the sun, hot and blazing, on my face and arms. I will look beautiful, I told myself, sun-tanned and beautiful.

A sound woke me. The click click of high heels on the wooden planking. Dazed, I opened my eyes and saw the woman standing in front of me. She was about five foot one, almost as wide as she was tall, and along with the outrageous false eyelashes, there was a red mouth like a scarlet wound in a seamed face and, over the bright red, a lip gloss. Her lower legs were surprisingly good, her skirt came just to above the knees. She had a bust like Pallas Athena. I didn't believe for one moment silicone. Silicone came later. This woman was circa the 1930's.

I guessed who she was. She was the landowner, the woman who rented her house to the Saxons. A taste for the grape. Her breath gave her away if nothing else did.

"Honey, I don't seem to know you," she said, squinting down.

"I'm Katherine Cornwall," I said, sitting up. "A friend of Janet's from New York."

"Hello there. Having fun?"

"Oh yes, it's delightful here."

"Swell."

She sat down, puffing a little. "My name's Lola Fischer. I mean, that's my real name. I was in the movies under another name. But it wouldn't mean anything to you, so why brag?"

"It *would,*" I said, earnestly. "Try me."

Her laugh was a snort. "Sure," she said, and extended a dramatic arm, with flab that hung from a sleeveless arm-hole like a ripe gourd. "So long, fame, I've had you, fame." Her voice was brassy. "All right, I used to act under the name Lola Montray. Mean anything to you?"

This time I really did sit up. Of course it meant something to me. To any movie buff. Lola Montray! Leading lady to George Brent and Paul Lukas and Ramon Navarro . . . Lola Montray!

Oh no, I thought, disillusioned. Not this stumpy lush.

I remembered the almond-shaped eyes, the splendid, bared shoulders, the creamy breasts. The zipped-in waist and the pearly teeth. And the hair, the raven hair.

"You're Lola Montray?"

"One and the same."

"Of course I would have recognized you. It's just that I was asleep. I've had too much sun."

Her laugh was a bray. "Little fool. Don't think you can kid me. So? What does it matter? I'm richer than God, and who cares what my teeth used to look like? Move over, honey, let me set. Tell that boy I'd like some grappa, some . . . let's put it plainly, some rye, unwatered, no ice cubes, four jiggers and fast. Got it?"

"Yes, Miss Montray," I said respectfully, and went inside to deliver Lola Montray's drink order.

"Her?" Gertrude said, clucking. "She here again? Don't fret yourself, Missy Kip, I get rid of her fast."

"But I don't mind at all, Gertrude. It's kind of fun. Don't worry."

"No no, you don't understand," she said, creases lining her brow. "She get drunk, flop, insensible, and somebody have to put her to bed. She stay sometimes three, four days, out of it."

"Oh?"

"Better we think up something," she said practically, and put a finger to her lip. "Let's see . . . we

97

can say Mr. Alex conducting at the Hollywood Bowl tonight. Go home fast, he have to practice." She looked hopefully at me. "Um hum?"

"But—"

"I know," she said, triumphantly. "The kids have scarlet fever. Yes? Quarantine. Dangerous. Send her home right away."

I left Gertrude thinking up dodges and went back to the sundeck. "We'll have something to drink right away," I said cordially. "How nice to meet you, Miss Montray."

"So you remember," she said, oozing satisfaction.

"Why, everybody knows you. Everyone who loves films."

"I had the best breasts in the business," she said serenely. "Those other sweater girls had wax pumped into them. Cheats, frauds. Tell me, did you see *Moonlight and Satan's Lover*?"

"Two or three times," I said. "I remember that scene when you came to the window and said, 'I am Columbina . . .'"

"You're a doll," she said rosily. "Where's our firewater?"

Just then Gertrude came out, with the firewater. "Oh, hello, Gert," Lola said, and reached for the glass. "How's Tom?"

"Tom as always," Gertrude said with dignity. "Feeling fine, Miss Lola?"

"Just swell. Good-bye. Thanks for the booze. I have a fan here I have to talk to."

Gertrude bowed out, her eyes cast heavenward, and Miss Montray and I talked. About the old days, before income tax, when you could pile up millions, and about Charlie Chaplin and Doug Fairbanks. About Lola, Lola, Lola . . .

"I had a big thing for . . ." I said once or twice, mentioning a male star's name.

"Sorry, honey, he was a bastard." Or, "Sorry, honey, he was a queer." Much of it was disillusioning, that was if I chose to believe her, but I was really having a high old time visiting with this star of yesteryear. Her drink was quickly gone and I said, "May I get you a refresher, Miss Montray?"

"Look," she said practically. "Just tell Slant-eyes to bring out the bottle, okay? They've got it in spades, these people, and I go easy on the rent, God knows, so leave her bring out a quart and I'll be my own bartender. All right, honey?"

"Yes, of course."

I hopped up and went inside to tell Gertrude. "See?" she said, excitedly. "Didn't I tell you?" She thrust a bottle of rye into my hands. "Never mind, I think of something."

I went back with the bottle, and Miss Montray reached for it with a look of glee. "Well, now we can get down to serious business," she said happily, and poured out a big one.

"And you, honey?"

"No, I'll nurse this one along."

"Well, you're young. You don't need it, or tranquilizers either. *I* do. Lots of us do. So? It's a nifty way to dig your grave."

And then the boys came out, on their way down to the beach, their tiny torsos bare and their lower quarters encased in minuscule swim trunks. Clearly, they were fond of their landlady. They both gave her a kiss,

99

and she opened a gigantic alligator bag and dug out some Blum's maple toffees. The children went down the wooden steps, tearing the wrappers off the candy.

"Adorable," Lola said, and told me she regretted not having given birth. "I did everything else, but not that." She made it sound like a major, super-publicity project, with big advertising and her name in lights: LOLA MONTRAY GIVES BIRTH TO A BOY . . . GIRLS . . . TWINS.

After a while I understood Gertrude's concern. The contents of the fifth went down, and down . . . and down. Miss Montray began to get quite tight. She had a little difficulty with certain words, and when the problem threw her she let her sentences dangle in mid-air. Her eyes grew glassy and once, when she got up to fill her glass, she almost fell onto the weathered floor of the sundeck.

"Oops," she said apologetically. "What was it I was saying?"

"About Errol Flynn."

"Oh, yes. No queer, he. What a man!"

"I guess so."

"I *know* so."

I asked her how long she had known the Saxons.

"Oh, years," she said. "They came here ten, fifteen years ago. He liked this house right away. I think it's a fright myself. I don't like out of style things. Right up to the minute, I believe in. I never lived in this crazy place. I own real estate all over; now that my looks are gone I'm glad I wasn't one of those dumb broads who threw it away with both hands. It's funny, but I always wanted to die right. Have my estate listed in the millions. That's the only asset an old woman can have.

100

These bums who tell you all a woman needs is a man are bananas. Women have a power drive too, and they better not forget it. I'm so rich I'm choking on it. That makes me feel real good, honey."

"I can understand that," I said, leading her back to the Saxons. "So you've known Alex and Janet for ten or fifteen years."

"Ever since they got married."

"Well, that's about . . . I guess thirteen or fourteen years."

She sighed. "Yup, they come and go, these damn long years." She swivelled in her seat and eyed me. "You know, aside from me I don't think they've made any real friends here. And you know whose fault that is when a couple doesn't mingle in the community. Not that there's much in the way of chintzy cookouts here or anything like that. But living in one place all the time wouldn't you think they'd have settled themselves *in*, so to speak?" She shook her head. "Of course I've always gotten along well with them." She dragged on a cigarette, coughed with that tight, choked cough that was the sign of a chain smoker, and looked narrowly at me.

"It's her, of course."

"Her?"

"Janet. It's the woman who sets the pace. Sometimes I feel damned sorry for him. Oh well, I don't suppose he's exactly dying to shoot the breeze with everyone and his brother, but Jeez, all that time and you oughta have some kind of give and take with this one and that one."

"But Miss Montray, they're both dedicated to their work, it being of a very special nature," I said, using

101

the phrase as an apologia to cover the entire situation. I was remembering my own question to Alex, last fall. *But doesn't she have any friends?*

Not really, he had said. *She has her work . . . and the children.*

She had more than that, I thought dryly. She had Howard, in San Francisco. She had that.

"Well, I'll tell you," Miss Montray said, "as Mimi puts it, they should have come to terms with their differences long ago. Of course she has her own axe to grind. But she's right. He's a man, with a man's needs and a man's right to a broader life than she sees fit to provide for him. Take me, for instance. I was married four times. Each one was different, naturally, so what does that mean? I have to be different for Tom, Dick and Harry. And the other one. All things to all men. Who does the compromising? The woman, of course."

"Who's Mimi?" I asked, breaking in.

She poured out some more firewater and lit another cigarette. "You must meet her, she's a good friend of mine. Alex's too. Oh, I could tell you things . . . now don't get me wrong. I'm not suggesting . . ."

She swallowed some liquor.

"But I happen to know that there was a time when she fully expected something from Alex. Oh, honey, that happens to all of us. And she was let down. You know? Well, wouldn't you be? If a man's wife left the scene, and he turned to you, and it looked like a split? Well, let me tell you, in all confidence, that she was mistaken. You see? Here they are, snug as a bug in a rug, even if it isn't all moonlight and roses. So she swallowed her bitterness and there she is, surviving.

102

Oh, well. I could tell you plenty of things like that, things that have happened to me . . ."

This long speech was so disjointed that I could make practically nothing of it. Except, of course, the innuendoes. All the pronouns . . . he, she. I didn't know to whom she was referring in all this: *she* swallowed her bitterness, *he* turned to *someone, she* was surviving.

But I was beginning to be most curious: if I could worm a few things out of Lola Montray I might get a few ideas sorted out. I leaned forward and started to frame a question and just then Gertrude came out of the house, saying that there was a telephone call for me.

"Urgent, New York on the line," she said, like a secretary. I thought it sounded terribly manufactured and I was also annoyed at the interruption, but Gertrude stood there like a martinet, with her arms folded, and there was nothing to do but make my apologies to Miss Montray.

She took it in good part, got up, weaving a little and held out a be-ringed hand like a grand duchess. "Such a pleasure," she said to me.

"Oh no, my pleasure," I said effusively, and Gertrude showed her out, a firm hand on her elbow. After a while there was the sound of an engine starting up out front and then Gertrude came back, chuckling.

"Missy?" She nudged me conspiratorially.

"*Is* there a telephone call for me?" I asked.

"No, no. Good excuse, though, yes? Ha ha! We got her out of our hair. Terrible woman. Drunk, finished, stupid. Want something to eat, Missy Kip?"

"Who's Mimi?" I asked.

"Mimi?"

But I saw her guarded eyes.

"Miss Montray mentioned someone called Mimi."

"I don't know. Maybe she dream it."

"Okay, never mind."

"I bring you some caviar."

"I don't want anything."

"Some buttered prawns."

"Thanks, no. Good heavens, Gertrude, I just had breakfast."

"Tom take you to Monterey? You spend golden afternoon?"

"Thanks, Gertrude. Tom doesn't have to bother. If I want, I can take a car. I was told I could."

"Yes, plenty of cars."

I followed her indoors. "Have you seen Janet this morning?"

"Yes, she go out. Over to her mother's. She be back soon."

Over to her mother's. It had an ominous sound. Supposing, after all, it *had* been Janet who had overheard my call to Norma. And how she was upset, talking it out with Mrs. Lance. I was sure now that it hadn't been Alex, as in view of our conversation he would almost certainly have said something.

I went up to my room and puttered, opening drawers and smoothing out lingerie and such. I felt a little fifth-wheelish, with the sounds of work coming from various rooms and no good morning greeting from Jan. I felt . . . out of place.

And then, as I had known I would, I went upstairs, quietly, to Janet's studio.

The beautiful, sun-lit room was marvelous. I thought of Jan saying, *This is where I live, Janet Lance* . . .

There were canvases stacked on the floor: I rummaged through them, looking at seascapes and skyscapes and paintings of the house. There were portraits as well; the children, and one of Fleur. And there was an indescribably appealing one of Tony. I didn't come across any of Alex, though, and it was odd, because there was also one of Zoltan, very well executed.

And then I found the terrible picture.

It was at the very back of a stack against the east wall, and I almost missed it because this particular pile of canvases was behind a door, a little door that, when opened, revealed a flight of steep steps that I knew must lead down to the kitchen regions below. A servant's flight of steps which was all that remained of former quarters for the help from another time.

I riffled through the canvases, not terribly interested at this point and then I saw it . . . and bent to it. And then pulled it out. I stood it upright and stared at it. And felt a surge of horror and cold distaste.

It was a very large canvas and I suppose it would have been classed as *l'art brut*. Black art. There was a small red fox, and it was being attacked by a large gray wolf, whose fangs sank deep into the flesh of the fox at the flank; the wolf's teeth were reddened with blood.

At the same time the wolf was set upon by a snarling hyena, whose muzzle tore open the hide of the wolf at the area of the vulnerable belly. The predations went on and on, an infinity of terrors: the hyena was mounted by a puma, whose claws raked crimson

105

streaks down the beast's back. The puma was the target for a male lion with a tawny mane; the lion was poised in the lower branches of a tree, ready to pounce.

At a far distance, drawn against the gentle, ineffable blue of a cerulean sky, a cow stood with reared head, its udder being devoured by a desert dog.

I stuffed it back in its place and left the room. The beautiful, bright room, with its secrets of the soul . . . Janet's soul.

And, in my own room again, sat on the edge of the bed, remembering the title Janet had given her picture, a title that had been scrawled across the very bottom of it, in a slanting stroke of a brush which had been dipped in bright vermilion . . . the color of fresh blood.

It was a terrible title for a painting like that.

The Meaning of Life.

Chapter 8

Janet got back to the house just before noon, and as soon as I saw her I knew that my fears about her being an unwitting listener to this morning's ill-fated telephone call to Connecticut were unfounded. She seemed in a very good mood, and apologized profusely for not having breakfasted with me.

"It was just that I wanted you to sleep, after my barging in on you last night, Kip. Not that any of us makes a ceremony over breakfast. We drift down whenever it's convenient for our schedules. It's only that it must have seemed frightfully inhospitable of me this first morning."

"No, that's all right," I said. "I reiterate that I don't want to stick out like a sore thumb in your busy lives. Don't give it another thought. I'd really dislike it if you thought you had to stand on ceremony. Please, Jan, let's . . . just do what we always did. Go our own ways. Or else I'll feel stiff and awkward."

"Well, we wouldn't want that," she said briskly.

"And yes, I told you to take one of the cars and show yourself around, but this morning I'm going to give myself a treat and go with you. I thought we'd go to Morro Bay."

"I'd love that . . . if it isn't taking you away from—"

"Nope. Today's a holiday. Okay?"

"Wonderful."

It was a scenic drive. There were rolling mountains and valleys, the latter with their pastel-colored houses dotting the hills up and down, and the fragrant eucalyptus trees casting their shade over all. Sheep huddled, grazing, in verdant pastures; there were, unpredictably, windmills, their giant arms whirling ponderously, and orchards with apple blossoms pink and white against the deep green of soft, rich grassland.

It was dream-like country, pierced by the Camino Real, with neat vineyards and pastures. There were swift flashes of color; the bright red of a lapwing in flight, the brilliant blue of lupines massed in a field, the deep purple of the grapes hanging heavily from trellises.

And then we were at Morro Bay, a brisk, lively port town with a smell of sea and fish. The famed rock was gargantuan, jutting up out of the peacock-blue water. Janet found a place to leave the car and we got out and walked. The Marina was jumping with activity; large and small craft were anchored at its edge and the divers were unloading their morning's catch. "One thing I do know," Janet said as we watched the fishermen. "I couldn't ever live far from the sea. It has such a fascination for me."

We watched a group of little kids who were following the activities of the man who was pulverizing the abalone steaks, tenderizing them with a great block of wood. He gave a whack to one side and then, flipping over the fish, gave a whack to the other side. And the children laughed, cheering.

"Give it a good one, Marcello," one little boy cried.

The Italian, a huge, curly-haired man with a bare, sweating torso, pounded the mallet. "Come here, I'll give you a taste of this thing," he teased, brandishing the mallet.

And there were mock-terrified screams.

We lunched at the Cambria Pines Lodge, an inn with the Victorian decor that had been so popular earlier in the century. I had my first abalone steak, finely-breaded and tender enough to cut with a fork. The taste of it resembled no other sea product I had ever eaten. I wasn't mad for it, but neither had I particularly enjoyed the Bouillabaise I'd had in Marseilles. Yet you eat what is indigenous to a region if you have any sense of adventure at all.

Afterwards, we visited an art gallery on the Main Street, and Janet introduced me to the proprietor. We all chatted about art and techniques and trends, and then the owner, a man named Walt Damon, served us espresso. It was getting on toward three o'clock when we left, to wander through other shops, Japanese places, with nets and shells and mutton-fat jade, other stores selling wicker and hand-blown glass and driftwood in exotic shapes.

It was in Ginny's Gift Shop that Janet ran into someone she knew. I was poking into some wicker barrels filled with India print scarfs. I thought about buying one or two to take back as gifts and then decided, how stupid, because you could pick up the identical items for the same price and perhaps less at dozens of places in Manhattan.

And then I heard someone say Janet's name and saw Jan's head turn around.

There was quite a long silence and I looked at Janet and saw her face freeze. Literally turn to stone. She stood, arrested in motion, and then she pulled herself together.

"Why, hello," she said, and her voice sounded funny.

The other woman, who was followed by a man who had an arm on hers, looked, to tell the truth, about as uneasy as Janet. She was about Jan's age, but going salt and pepper and her face had that leathered look that comes from outdoor living. She was a suburban type, dressed in a drip-dry sheath in a rather undistinguished print, and her hands were clasped together as if she didn't know what to do with them.

I knew, instantly, that this unexpected meeting of the two women was welcome to neither of them.

"How are you?" the strange woman asked, with a stiff smile.

"Just fine. And you, Anne?"

"Very well!

Janet introduced me, quietly, and we spoke for a few more minutes, just trivial stuff, the way people do who haven't seen each other in a long time.

And then everyone said, "Good-bye, have a nice day."

Janet and I left the shop and went on walking.

I knew that, for some reason I couldn't fathom, the meeting in that shop had upset and irritated Janet.

One didn't ask, naturally, but I tried to think of something to do or say that would get her mind off the people we had just met. And as we passed a small concession, where you could, for a quarter, shoot moving targets, I said I would like to try my luck.

"Okay," Jan said, obviously trying to recover herself.

I put down my quarter and picked up a gun. I didn't hit anything, and then I put another quarter down and told Janet to take a stab at it. She looked unseeingly at the counter and said no, thank you, so I picked up the gun again and this time I rang the bell with a sure shot.

"Well, this is a lucky little lady," the barker said, and pointed to a shelf with prizes, all hideous, cheap china and warped glass and ghastly paperweights with snow sifting down inside them.

Out of some perverse whim I chose a terrible-looking little doll with a painted face, stiff hair and jointed limbs.

Its eyes closed when you laid it down, and eyelashes, spiky and blond, swept the rouged cheeks.

Janet smiled vaguely. "You nut," she said. "What do you want with that grotesque thing?"

"Since I've neither chick nor child this will be a surrogate," I said, trying to interest and amuse her. And we walked along further, with me cradling the hideous doll in my arms. To get a rise out of Janet I talked to it, saying foolish things like, "Now you behave, you little monster. If you don't stop crying you'll get Spam for supper."

She did laugh, but she still looked white-faced and preoccupied. Should I come right out and ask her why

111

she was so upset about meeting that woman? Or should I let it lie?

I let it lie. Years ago Janet had had an abortive love affair with a local Amherst boy, and it had broken up. I never had known what happened . . . probably her mother, since the boy was ill-favored in his background. But I remembered that she had suffered silently, and no one, not Norma, not I, had dared to ask . . . or offer sympathy. She was like that, keeping things to herself.

I just thought it was a dismal coincidence that we had had to meet that old acquaintance, for that woman, named Anne Kaufman, had brought to mind, quite obviously, something Janet wanted to forget, the way she had wanted to forget her sad love affair with Leon Bryant.

And from then on, all the way home, she scarcely spoke. We drove the eighty mile stretch of highway between Cambria and Carmel, one of the most incredibly scenic routes in the U.S., in almost total silence. Janet drove much too fast, and the hairpin turns, climbs, plummeting drops, frightened me. One badly-negotiated turn and we'd plunge down . . . and down, and down.

The beaches below, silver with warped cypresses that were like bonzai trees, were brilliant with jasper, agate, moonstones and jade. If we hit a rock, or a road barrier, we would die buried in beauty, plunge into the glaring blue waters below. And there was one heart-stopping moment when I was almost sure that was Janet's intention.

I had my feet braced on the floor. I looked down at my hands, gripping the seat; the knuckles were white.

And then she zoomed the car into a narrow dirt road that appeared suddenly. Gravel spit up a few seconds later, and we were at a small lookout point that had been built to accommodate sight-seeing cars, though there were none there at the moment.

She braked sharply, and we came to a stop.

"Wanna go down to the sea?" she asked.

"It's a long way, isn't it?"

"Chicken?"

"No, certainly not. Okay, let's go down."

I left the doll sitting stupidly in my place, her tiny mouth bee-stung and painted a ghastly red. Then Janet locked the car and we made our way downwards, through furze and sea grass and tangled trees.

"You can see why they loved this place," Janet called to me over her shoulder. "Robinson Jeffers and Edward Weston. The artistic mind *is* different," she said, insisting. "Whoever disputes that is a horse's backside."

"I agree with you."

I certainly did.

We at last came to the bottom. The cliff, from which we had just come, was rockbound and shaly, stern and timeless, and the sea throbbed at our feet, angry, tumultuous, spraying us. A spit of land, rocky and gray, lay ahead, placing us in a kind of semi-circular cove. Bent pines, weathered and white, were like crippled limbs, and the bleached driftwood sprawled on the pebbly beach.

"Let's wade," Jan suggested.

We pulled off our sandals and held up our dresses and scrabbled in the water, dashing back every few seconds as a new wave broke. We were both laughing, and I thought, oh, Janet's all right again, and that we were like two children with not a care in the world.

And then, just as a great breaker smashed in to threaten us, I started racing shoreward again, but Janet just stood there, looking at the foaming, churning wave . . . and then it was almost upon her.

"Hey," I shrieked. "Janet, you fool . . ."

She stood there for one fraction of a second longer, and I raced back to her.

"Janet."

Before I could get to her she turned, all at the last moment, and dashed, fled. But she was drenched with the spume, her hair streaming, her lashes wet and long and dark. She plodded back a ways, away from the churning water, and dropped onto the sand.

"I almost got mine then, didn't I?" she asked.

Even a superb swimmer wouldn't have had much chance in all that turbulence. I didn't say anything, though my heart was racing, and soon Jan began laughing again, pulling out her dress where it stuck to her and trying to fluff out her matted, wet hair.

I laughed too, but my heart wasn't in it. Because I knew I would never quite forget her standing there, stock still, facing that oncoming wall of water. As if she were welcoming it, as if she was asking it to claim her . . .

And yet, when the sun had dried her fairly well, and we climbed back up and got in the car again, she was serene again, and she didn't reach constantly for a cigarette. She seemed calm somehow, somehow peaceful, as if something had been resolved in her mind. She said amusing things, too, like "I just washed my hair and I can't do a thing with it," while twisting it, drolly, into ridiculous shapes.

"The bride of Frankenstein, that's me," she said, and once reached over to pat my doll on its bottom.

"Shut up, you silly bitch," she said. "You say mama once more and I'll give you what for, you little bugger."

And for the first time since I had arrived in California, Janet seemed to be completely herself again. That forced gaiety, that brittle quality vanished and suddenly, as if by legerdemain, my friend was the way she had always been. Calm, quiet, smiling, with a rich lode of sly humor. It was as if the stranger had vanished and the woman I had always known had come back.

She insisted on treating my silly doll as a guest. "Kip has a friend visiting her," she told everyone when we were having drinks. "Darling, for goodness' sake, why isn't she *here* with us, partaking?"

"What does Mama mean, Kip?"

I laughed. "I was good with my aim at a shooting gallery," I said. "I won a prize."

"Show the boys," Janet said, and I had to get up and trot upstairs for the painted doll Plaintively, she cried when I laid her back in my arms. The boys were delighted, and there was a contest for a name for her. Zoltan sat her in his lap and suggested Mae West. Fleur thought Barbarella and Tony came up with Daisy Mae.

But in the end she was called Olympia, Alex's contribution, and when he told his kids about the sequence from "Tales of Hoffmann," in which the me-

115

chanical doll, Olympia, dances herself to death for the sake of her lover, Hoffmann, the choice was made.

"She has a pale and pasty look," Zoltan remarked. "Get those frilly clothes off her, Kip, and put her in a bathing suit. She needs a good sun-tan."

"She needs a better brand of make-up," Janet said. "That red-lipped look went out in the Forties."

"Oh no, she's *pretty*," Roger insisted, sticking up for poor Olympia.

After the cocktail hour we ate down on the beach, a picnic supper; needless to say the boys were beside themselves, screeching in their treble voices, and they helped their father gather driftwood for a roaring fire. The evening quickly became chilly, but the fire warmed our bones and lit the growing darkness.

Afterwards we sang. It was Janet who started us off.

"Tenting tonight, tenting tonight, tenting on the old camp ground . . ."

We sang "Beautiful Dreamer", "Aurelie", "Shenendoah." I discovered, charmed, that Alex Junior had an ear for the second part. These things were born in you; true, with perfect pitch, he complemented the melody, and was happy as a lark when I told him God had given him a nice present.

"I don't know how I do it," he said, looking up at me. "It just comes out of my head."

"You don't have to think about it," I said. "It's inside you, and is a very nice thing to have."

"Is that the same God who punishes you if you're naughty?" Roger asked seriously.

"There's only one God," I said. "For everyone. And if you're naughty it's your parents who must punish you. God is too busy arranging the seasons."

"Oh, is that what He's up to," Alex said, mildly. He threw another piece of wood on the fire. "I always thought he spent his time gazing down at us, amazed and fascinated, through a kind of microscope. You know . . . what are these Lilliputians doing, for goodness' sake."

"Lilliputians?" Roger repeated, interested. "That's *Gulliver's Travels*. Is God in that too?"

"God isn't a man at all," Alex Junior insisted. "He's a spirit, that's what he is. You can never see him, only feel him." He raised a skyward finger. "Heaven isn't up there," he said scornfully. "Outer space is up there. God is love."

"Oh?" Roger said uncertainly. "But where does he live?"

"That's a silly thing to say," his brother said strictly, and I thought it was only because he had no answer. "He isn't a human being, you know. He lives everywhere. In a leaf, a spiderweb."

"In a spiderweb?" Roger echoed, awed. "A little place like that?"

"Not really in a spiderweb, you nut. It was only a figure of speech."

"Here endeth the reading of the Lesson," Alex said dryly, and handed me a snifter of brandy. "This will take the chill away, Katherine."

The cognac slid, burning, warming, down my gullet. The fire blazed away, blue flames leaping up into the sky. All around me were the voices of friends, soothing, companionable. I knew I'd have to go home some time. This was only an idyllic hiatus. But the thought of leaving all this, the sea and sand and the timeless roar of the waters, the exciting Pacific coast, my friends, the children, made me want to weep.

The tide washed up, licking at our feet now. The breakers rose, toweringly, sounding like a dirge, as the spray misted over us, and the children retreated, shrieking, while the salt wet splashed over them, their tiny bodies, vulnerable, tender, so small, so small.

Chapter 9

I didn't see Janet all morning on the following day, and when I ran into Zoltan at one point he told me she was in San Francisco.

Thoughts are visual: at once there arose in my mind a vision of that row house on Ghiradelli Square. Like an unbidden mirage. A second later Zoltan went on to explain that Janet did welfare work for a Catholic philanthropic society.

"The Little Sisters of the Poor," he said.

We talked for a while and then Zoltan went back to his room because he was "knocking off" an article about the Hungarian hinterlands and their old-world customs which to this day, he told me, were observed in certain regions.

"I thought I might sell it to *Holiday Magazine*," he said.

I wished him luck, although privately I happened to feel that it wasn't so easy to sell to the magazines, since most of them were planned long in advance and had their own staff writers, but if it gave him pleasure, and hope, I was all for it. He was undoubtedly an experienced and learned man in a world of mediocrities whose work was sadly lacking in originality and erudition and the eternal verities. But the latter part of the 20th century, I very often decided, was a rather discouraging time for an artist of any kind to live in.

Particularly someone who wasn't young any more.

I thought about going down to the beach, but changed my mind. I don't know why I came to my final conclusion, but at any rate it was for that matter quite impulsive. I had a pre-lunch drink, which Tom made for me, and it was a stiff one. Afterwards I went inside and asked Gertrude where the Little Sisters of the Poor was.

"Where Missy Janet go? Yes," she said. "Masonic Street."

"Thanks, Gertrude. I'm going to take the Triumph. I thought I might go to St. Simeon."

"That's a beautiful place," she said, rolling her eyes in ecstasy. "See it, Kip. All those pools, statues . . . a million rooms. Beautiful."

She told me to get the keys from Tom.

It was a clear, cloudless day and I crossed the Expressway at about two o'clock, and came soon after that to Ghiradelli Square.

And there were the row houses, where that fairhaired man lived. Howard. I drove slowly past the pretty little stone buildings and suddenly saw what I had half expected to find.

A familiar car, a bright blue Dauphine.

I recognized the license plate.

I drove on.

I didn't need any other confirmation. Janet wasn't doing welfare work, as Zoltan had claimed. No, she was spending an afternoon, an illicit afternoon, in Ghiradelli Square, with Howard something or other.

I drove aimlessly, around and around and up and up, seeing the sights of the city only subliminally, because I was so disturbed and . . . yes, angry.

After a while I thought, if Janet professed to be engaged in good works with an organization named the Little Sisters of the Poor, then there must be some grain of truth in that, at least. Because if someone really wanted to prove it, then Janet would certainly have to have some affiliation with that organization. And so, even if she wasn't there now, she must be known there, must show up occasionally.

I asked a street cop how to get to Masonic Street, and was directed.

I stopped the car in front of a red brick building, very baroque, with cupolas and a porte cochere, six stories in height. It was set well back from the street and nicely planted.

Inside there was a fresh-faced young girl in coif and habit, who acted as receptionist. Could she help me, she asked.

"I'm not sure," I said. "I wondered . . . well, you see, a friend of mine, Mrs. Saxon, is doing some volunteer work today. I thought it would be nice if I could help her."

"Oh yes, Mrs. Saxon," she said. "But I'm afraid you were mistaken. She isn't here today."

"Oh, I'm sorry. Then I guess you're right. I must have misunderstood."

"Of course she might come later on."

"But did you expect her?"

"Oh no, not really. There is no schedule, no routine. Our volunteers help out when they can. I hope she does come today, because there's a shortage of mothers." She smiled explanatorily. "We call them mothers, you see, and Mrs. Saxon is very good with children."

"I see."

What else could I say? The girl started to go on, but I waved a negative hand. "No, it's all right. If she does show up, better not say anything, Sister. You see . . ."

I bent forward confidentially. I was suddenly aghast at what I'd done. Pried into Janet's private life, followed her into San Francisco.

She wouldn't like that. No one would. Especially someone who, instead of doing charitable work as advertised, was spending an erotic afternoon with a lover.

"You don't mind," I said resolutely. "Just don't mention I was here. You don't mind? It might be . . . very . . ."

I cleared my throat. I was beginning to feel moist and uncomfortable. "It's just that . . . well, she might think—"

The girl raised an understanding face. "It's all right," she said. "It doesn't matter. Please don't worry. I won't say anything, my dear sister in God. Go your way in peace."

Her smile was as sweet as honey, *really* sweet, a good, Christian smile. "And have a good day," she said, as I moved away from the desk. "If you're hungry, there's a fine restaurant nearby. Inexpensive and with good food. The Chanticleer. I recommend it highly."

"Thank you," I said, and went out. The sun, after the dim interior of the sanctuary, was blinding.

I didn't go to the Chanticleer. I wasn't hungry, in the first place. I got in the car and drove about, sniffing the salty air. And finally, telling myself I was surely going off the deep end, I found a parking space and went into a drugstore where there was a phone booth and directories. I got out the phone book. I had decided to look up the woman I'd met with Janet at Morro Bay. Kaufman was the name . . . David . . . Daniel? The introduction had been hasty and awkward. Kaufmans. And there was a Daniel . . . a good bit for a first trip.

The phone rang for a long time and then at last, just as I was about to give up, it was answered. A woman's voice said hello.

"Mrs. Kaufman?"

"Yes," she said.

A funny little thrill ran through me. I recognized the voice. This was the same woman, I was sure.

I said, "Is this the Mrs. Kaufman I met at Morro Bay with Janet Saxon?"

There was a long, long silence. And then:

"Yes, it is," she said.

"Then you remember me. Katherine Cornwall? I was afraid I might have the wrong number."

"No, you have the right number," she said, and then added, not so much lamely as quietly and with a kind of resignation, "Hello."

"Hello, I'm so sorry to bother you, Mrs. Kaufman.

You see, I happen to be in San Francisco. I just wondered . . . if it's not too much of an inconvenience for you . . . might I stop in and say hello?"

The wires hummed and I waited. And then at last, as if she couldn't resist it, the woman said, "Yes, certainly. I have scotch in the house, and I think some gin."

"I'd as soon have coffee," I said.

She gave me directions, adding, "It's the house with the blue shutters."

I was in front of the house with the blue shutters three quarters of an hour later.

She opened the door. She was in a neat little housecoat, buttoned down the front, and her hair was freshly done. She smelled of something wholesome . . . Yardley's, perhaps . . . and her feet were tidily slippered. And she did the most unexpected thing when she closed the door behind me.

She leaned forward and put her lips quickly to my cheek.

She seated me on a cretonne-covered couch, and on a coffee table there was a bottle of gin and another of J and B. There was also the aroma of fresh coffee trickling in from other rooms.

I said the coffee smelled wonderful, and that was what we had.

When she had filled our cups and passed a plate of cookies to me an awkward silence fell on us. I could see that she was ill at ease (God knew *I* was), and I quickly broke the lapse by saying how nice her house was.

"Would you care to see the rest of it?" she asked.

"That's . . . very kind of you."

She showed me around, and it was evident that this little, modest split-level was her castle. It was not in bad taste, simply undistinguished, and as neat as a pin. I knew her neighbors must say about her that you could eat off Mrs. Kaufman's floor.

When we sat down again I felt less ill at ease. "It must seem very odd to you," I said. "I mean, my coming here . . . a stranger."

"I didn't . . . don't know what to think," she said, but there was a queer kind of expectancy on her face, as if she sensed drama and, perhaps, needed it. Her eyes were waiting and bright and, occasionally, she put a finger against her two top front teeth.

And I started talking. About Janet, and when I was young, and how she had guided me and nurtured me. "You see," I finished, "I know there's something wrong in her life . . . and I had hoped to find out something . . . from . . ."

"From anyone," I said with a tight smile. "Anyone who might shed light on her problems." She started to say something but I went quickly on. "Because I have the feeling that she's going down for the third time, and if I can prevent that . . ."

I shifted in my chair. I was doing this very badly, I thought.

"You see, when I saw you and Janet meet, and both of you weren't too pleased about it . . ."

My God, what the hell am I doing here? I asked myself, as a clock ticked loudly, and a cat meowed from somewhere in the back regions.

"Could you tell me anything about Janet that might help me?" I asked desperately. "Because I can't stay here forever. I have to go home . . . some time . . ."

She waited a long time before answering, looking at me with an indescribable expression. It was such a long time that I began to sweat, really sweat, and when a leaf dropped off a begonia plant on the table alongside me, I nearly jumped out of my skin. Then she said, with a queer look on her face, "No. I can't. I'm sorry about it, too. But you see, I also have things to forget. And when I ran into Janet again, after all those years, and that dreadful sadness, I realized that it will never leave me, what I did and what she did."

She put a hand over her mouth.

"But what does that mean?" I asked, leaning forward.

She was obviously wrestling with herself, and her face mirrored her inner struggle. The hand pressed against her neat mouth and then came away again, fell down by her side.

"I can only tell you this," she said at last. "Janet and I, at a certain point in our young lives, had a common tragedy. We shared our grief, confided in each other, and then went our separate ways. Seeing her again brought it all back, and I expect it was the same for her."

She undid one of the buttons on the front of her dress, fiddled with it and then buttoned it again. "You're a nice girl, a good, loving friend, and for that I respect you. But Janet will solve her problems in her own way. As I've had to do."

Her rather ordinary, suburban, pragmatic facade was suddenly dignified by a kind of beauty. "To have a friend like you," she said, "must be very nice. I'm glad to have had you for a visitor, Miss Cornwall, and I'll remember you."

I knew I was being dismissed. She had told me nothing, would tell me nothing . . . and she wanted me to go now. But that she had meant what she said, I could tell by her wistful eyes. That she envied Janet her solicitous, meddling friend.

But she did so much for me, I wanted to protest. Without Janet in my formative years I might have amounted to nothing, nothing at all.

I got up. "It's been a real pleasure to be with you," I said, holding out my hand. "And I wish you the best, the very best."

"I wish you the same," she said, as she saw me to the door. She was waving as I pulled out of the driveway, and she was just a nonentity, a woman with a small life, but I drove away remembering her brave eyes, and I was thinking that what was hidden in a person's breast didn't show on the outside, and that this was a good, courageous woman. Who had, with Janet, shared a common tragedy.

What was that tragedy?

I was home at about five o'clock. Janet was home too; her car was parked with the others.

I ran into Alex, who asked me if I'd had a pleasant day, and then saw the three kids, Tony and Fleur and Dennis, on their way to the sundeck. "Where' you been?" Tony asked and, without waiting for an answer, followed his friends.

Zoltan waddled down the stairs and I said yes, I'd be right down, as soon as I'd freshened up a bit.

I went up to my room and looked out the window where the voices rose from the sundeck. Jan's two little boys were sitting on the glider, the doll Olympia beside them, and Roger was holding a straw to her mouth so that she could drink a bottle of coke.

Janet?

She wasn't down there. Everyone else was. Except for Janet and her friend Kip.

We're the two odd ones, I thought dolefully. Janet and I.

I showered, dried, and changed into ducks and a shirt. And then looked down to the sundeck again. I counted them. Janet wasn't among them.

Resolutely, I climbed the stairs to her studio.

The door was ajar, but even before I got to it I heard her voice.

A wave of revulsion swept over me. She was talking to *him* again.

She had just spent the day with him, but that was not enough. Now she was on the phone.

I was just about to turn away, numbed, when I heard her say her own name. Softly, eerily . . . there was something weird about it. It didn't sound as if she were talking on the telephone. It sounded . . . different.

On an impulse I turned back, pushed open the door of her studio a slight bit, and gazed in. And then I saw her.

She was sitting, her profile toward me, at a long mirror on one wall. It crossed my mind, as I watched her, that she used the mirror for self portraits. At any rate, she was sitting in front of it and was leaning forward, studying herself in the glass.

And she was saying something.

I almost turned away again. Almost . . . but because there was something so striking about the way she sat there, leaning forward and looking at her reflection, I stayed, waiting.

She was talking softly. Her lips were moving, and she was saying something in a muted voice. I strained my ears . . . and then I heard her say, distinctly, "Janet. I am Janet. I am Janet. Janet."

Prickles rose on my skin. I stared, wide-eyed. Through the slit in the door I watched my oblivious, unwitting friend talk to herself in the mirror, staring into the glass, piteously insisting on her own identity.

Suddenly her arm went up, tore at her hair, swept it across her face wildly, until she had hidden from herself her own reflection. A shudder ran through her. She didn't cry. She simply sat there blinded by her own hair, an unweeping Niobe.

Numb with shock, I quietly withdrew. There was no question of going to her. How much I wanted to rush in and confront her . . . but to invade that terrible, agonized moment would have been unthinkable.

The house was silent. All the activity, all the life, all the warmth was outdoors. I heard no voices, no sounds at all. The house seemed deserted, hushed, was like a tomb, a tomb in which my friend, Janet, was imprisoned.

Chapter 10

Two days later the strange car was parked down the road.

I discovered it quite by accident. The thing was that I had tired of the beach, as Janet had told me I would, and also of the "sameness" she had complained of. I was by now as brown as a walnut, had wearied of the sundeck, the beach, the landscape, and needed desperately to *walk*.

People who live outside cities scarcely ever walk. They get into cars and drive to supermarkets. City folk leave their front doorstep and leg it, along Madison, Lex, Third and such. They do their food shopping on foot, lugging brown paper parcels, hotfoot down to Bloomingdale's for that scarf or that sweater, and before you knew it, if you lived in a large city like mine, New York, you found you had walked several miles in the course of a day.

I missed that.

I was, after all, eating heartily, lying about suntanning, gaining pounds and getting, not very, but just a little bit bored. Not that you could be bored for very long in the company I was keeping, with the variety of personalities in the household. Zoltan was a joy, feeding me "instant history" piecemeal, Tony and Fleur were good little companions once their day's studies were over and the two little boys, with their piping voices, had captured my heart.

And Janet . . . well, I still loved her, very much.

But for most of the day they were all occupied. While I took ocean dips, ate snacks on the sundeck and was, essentially, a lotus eater, the rest of them were hard at work.

And so I started taking hikes. Climbing up the road, which was a main highway, and discovering little side paths that led nowhere in particular, but which were pretty, foresty, with a wealth of wild flowers. I picked blossoms which I later arranged in large crystal vases to the delight and admiration of everyone else, strode through knee-high grassy fields and pushed my way through branch and leaf, discovering hidden dells here and there.

And on this particular day, returning from one of my wild foragings abroad, I saw the small car parked in a culvert. I wonder whose car that is, I thought, and then almost forgot about it as I walked back to the house. I went in and got some vases from Gertrude and played around with fancy, Oriental-type arrangements. Fleur came down while I was doing this, in a bikini, with a body like a young goddess, and said come on down to the beach. The kids were there, and Mr. Saxon, because she really *knew* the Mendelssohn now, had dismissed her for the day. We could play Botticelli.

Botticelli was a word game popular with the Saxons.

"Fine," I said. "Just as soon as I finish this."

"You are *so* artistic," she cried, and left me.

I finished my self-appointed job after half an hour or so, washed my hands in the kitchen, gossiping a bit with Gertrude, and then went outside and started down the wooden steps. From the top I could see Fleur, stretched out on her stomach, and the two little boys seemed to be trying to push potato chips into my doll Olympia's mouth.

Oh, poor Olympia, I thought and suddenly changed my mind about going down to the beach. I don't know . . . I was restless, somehow, I wanted to be by myself. It was nothing more than that, certainly not a premonition of any kind. It was just nothing, nothing at all, that made me walk, instead, out the side of the house and meander aimlessly along.

I was in bare feet and the ground, soft and loamy, hid whatever noise I may have made. And suddenly I heard a sound.

It was an odd sound . . . a kind of click, and then I saw someone through a screen of bushes. I thought at first that it must be Dennis, because there was a flash of fair hair, and was about to retrace my steps, not keen on chinning with that self-pitying boy, when I caught sight of a much taller figure. Not with the slight stature of young Dennis, but someone bigger, more substantial. And, pausing, I pulled aside branches and saw . . .

The man from San Francisco.

I was, to put it mildly, astonished. So he came here? Drove out from San Francisco and lurked about? I was asking myself why when I heard the click again and, as the bushes parted to give me a clear view of him, I saw that he was—from the vantage point of the rise on which he stood—aiming a camera down at the beach. And I saw too that he had just snapped a picture.

I followed his eyes, where his eyes were focused, and I could see, in my field of vision and his, the children down there on the sand, Roger and Alex Junior, with Fleur, in her turquoise bikini.

I stood perfectly still. He adjusted his camera again, and the shutter clicked once again. Then he turned the knob and again the click came.

What the devil was that man from San Francisco doing?

Taking pictures of Janet's children, that was clear . . . but why? For what purpose? And with his car hidden in a side road . . . and supposing himself all alone and unobserved?

Just then he lowered his camera, made some adjustment to it, and was raising it again when a tiny twig snapped off the branch I was holding, with a sharp twang. Instantly the man named Howard reared up his head and saw me there.

I must say that my reflexes were fine. I threw down the branch, which was dry and dead in my hand and stepped out from my place of concealment with an easy smile. I nodded, the way strangers outside of urban centers nod to other strangers, and said in a voice that surprised me with its blithe and calm friendliness that it was a lovely day, wasn't it?

For a second he was voiceless, and I knew he was shaken at finding himself discovered. It was more than obvious that he was far from pleased. And then finally he spoke.

"Yes, a nice day," he said, and his voice was deep, a rich baritone, but with a curiously dead quality.

"This is such a lovely spot, isn't it?" I said.

"Lovely, yes."

"It's so stupid I didn't bring a camera," I went on. "I'm from New York, but I didn't bring a camera. That was stupid, wasn't it?"

"You could rent one," he said.

"Yes, I suppose so."

And then I nodded again, and after a short interim he nodded back, then slung his camera over his shoulder and walked off, climbing the hill, disappearing after a while behind a stand of trees. I could hear the thud of his footsteps and the swish of leaves as he made a way for himself through the woods. A short while later I heard the motor of a car start up, and then silence.

I stood there and thought. Taking pictures of Janet's little boys . . . for what reason?

I found I didn't want to think any further than that. There was nothing wrong with my imagination, except that it was hyperactive. Just take it easy, I told myself. Just take it easy, and don't jump to idiotic conclusions.

But I was inordinately relieved to see Alex on the sundeck when I got back to the house. And to make it easier for me, he was alone.

135

I started off by making some small talk and then I scrapped it and said, baldly, "Alex, I want to tell you something."

"Oh?" He looked up, alerted by the seriousness of my tone.

"There was someone on the grounds here."

"Who?"

"A man. I saw his car first. It was parked near that stand of cypresses, just off the main road."

"So?"

"He was taking pictures."

"A photographer?"

"Alex, don't think I'm . . . it seemed to me that he was taking pictures of your children. Alex and Roger."

"But why?"

"I don't know. It just . . . seemed odd to me. A stranger, and—"

At that moment Zoltan stepped out onto the sundeck, his fleshy legs clad in knee-length shorts. I could have killed him; for the first time I was sorry to see his large, ponderous frame heave into view.

Alex raised a hand in abstracted greeting and bade me go on. Zoltan hesitated, seeing our gravity of mood. Alex smiled, shrugged, said, "It's all right, Zoltan. Kip and I were just talking about something she saw awhile ago."

And to me he said, "Go on, Kip. What is it that's on your mind?"

"It's just that . . . I felt funny about it. Seeing him stare down at the beach, at the children, and then snap those pictures. Why would he do that? I mean . . . oh, I realize it sounds neurotic . . . but he seemed so intent on getting your children on film.

136

And I can't really see why. I mean—"

Alex looked peculiarly at me. "Why does it disturb you so much?"

I had to hedge. I couldn't say, "Because he's Howard, that man your wife goes to see in San Francisco."

I couldn't say that!

I had to compromise. "Because, I don't know why, but it did," I said lamely.

He thought it over. "I see," he said at last.

"Isn't this a private beach and property?" I persisted.

"Yes, more or less. But the entire terrain isn't sacrosanct. And it's not even trespassing, legally speaking, for someone to go down there and swim. Let's put it this way . . . if I found a stranger using the beach roundabouts, I wouldn't call my lawyer. I'd simply tell that stranger that I would prefer it if he picked another spot. Kip, the waterfront is, substantially, in the public domain. The acreage surrounding the house here is, of course, private property."

"This wasn't on the beach, it was on the acreage surrounding the house," I said stubbornly.

"Oh. Well," Alex said reasonably, "I wouldn't worry about it. It was just someone enjoying this delicious countryside. Anyone would want to do the same thing. Take all the pictures he could. It's of such wondrous beauty. Certainly I can understand—"

Gertrude came to the door just then and said that there was a call for Mr. Saxon, please. And Alex got up and went right into the house.

I sat looking out at the water, troubled, and Zoltan, seeing my anxiety, questioned me. "What's wrong?" he asked. "You are unhappy about some incident?"

137

"Yes, quite."

"What is it?"

"You heard me talking to Alex. There was this stranger taking pictures of their kids down on the beach. Only it *wasn't* a stranger. I mean . . . not really. It was a man I've seen before."

"Really?" He leaned toward me, his eyes alert and interested. "But if it wasn't a stranger, then what's the problem?"

I looked nervously toward the house, but Alex had vanished. And I came out with it. "This man wasn't really a stranger," I said again. "I know who he is."

"You do?"

"Yes. He lives in San Francisco. I saw him the first day I arrived. He was with Janet. He lives there, in San Francisco, in Ghiradelli Square. And—"

I fell silent. I was thinking. That camera aimed at the beach. The lens registering it . . . Jan's two children.

Zoltan came over to me. "But you must get this off your mind," he said. His face was very serious and sympathetic. "Why didn't you tell Mr. Saxon this?"

"I can't!"

"But why?"

"It's only a guess," I said agitatedly. "But I think he and Janet . . . no, I won't say more . . . except his taking pictures of Jan's children . . . what can that *mean*?"

"You really think he was taking pictures of Roger and Alex?"

"I saw him! He clicked the shutter and then again . . . and again. They were down there, on the beach, the two boys, with Fleur."

138

"But what for?"

Zoltan's face was quizzical, as if to laugh off my fears. My fears?

Kidnaping. Why should I think of such a thing? Because I was hysterical, neurotic? Or because, since I had come out here, my senses had sharpened to the point that I *could* think such a thing . . . without any valid reason for it . . .

Kidnaping.

Am I going crazy? I thought.

Zoltan leaned back in his chair and drained his beer glass. His face was calm and comfortable and not in the least censorious. He didn't laugh at me, or scoff at my vapors. He simply said, "I wonder why we always think the worst? I mean, Kip, not just you, but all of us. That we invent imaginary disasters and fantastic dooms . . ."

He put his glass down on the table and smiled.

"Why not forget it and relax? These are peaceful climes. If any place is innocent of evil and evil intent, this is. So don't nag yourself with useless and baseless worries." His dear, sweet smile made me feel foolish and silly. "Are you going to lose sleep over this?" he asked drolly.

"No, no," I said, realizing that Zoltan, from his unworldly, *removed* point of view could never understand the undercurrents that were boiling in the household, that only I could know about. "It's all right, Zoltan. I won't think about it again. I've told Alex, and that's all I can do. Let me think about it."

"But you just said you wouldn't think about it again! "

I laughed. "Well, I'm a woman. Aren't women supposed to have the prerogative of changing their minds?"

And we talked for a while; I could see he was trying to get my mind off what he clearly considered baseless worries. But it was later on that same day that a second peculiar incident happened. It was just before the cocktail hour, and I was strolling along the beach, all by myself, because to tell the truth this was the hour I liked best on the sands, with the sun sinking beyond the horizon and a beautiful cool breeze sweeping the coast.

And then, damn it, I heard Dennis' voice.

He caught up to me, said "Hi," and, resignedly, I answered his greeting. We walked side by side, but he didn't gab this time; he was almost silent except for once, when I stepped on a sharp shell and said, "Ouch," he reached out and caught hold of me.

"What is it?"

"Nothing. I cut my foot a bit, that's all."

He bent down and looked at it. There was only a very little bit of blood, but he made me wet it in the water. "The salt will heal it," he said.

Later, a breaker caught me unawares, splashing me and dampening my shirt. Dennis watched as I tried to palm myself dry, and then he said, in a kind of breathless voice, "How about a little dip?"

"What?"

"Let's get really wet. It'll be cold as hell. But it will take the kinks out of you."

I gave him a quizzical look. "In this?" I ran my hands down my shirt and pants.

"Take them off."

"How amusing."

"What's so funny? Let's strip down and go for a quick swim."

I gave him a level glance. "You do your thing," I said. "Don't mind me. I'll turn my back."

He didn't answer. He just stood there and pulled off his shirt, stepped out of his leather sandals and walked a little way into the foaming surf. "It's nice," he said. "Come on, let's skinny dip."

"Thanks just the same."

"I ain't going to twist your arm," he muttered. "Suit yourself."

"I will."

He walked a little further into the ocean. "It's the best scene there is," he called back, and I saw his pectoral muscles ripple. He started back and joined me again. "Sensation is everything," he said ringingly, and his eyes challenged mine. "Right?"

"No, wrong," I said.

"Stake your claim. Tell me why it's not everything and I'll prove you wrong."

"Okay." I was determined not to show my annoyance. "Babies are *all* sensation. They enjoy the primitive comforts of milk, caresses, the functions of their own tiny bodies. But that's juvenile. Later, there comes the awareness of a more profound meaning to existence. Sensation in itself is animalistic. It has to be aligned with other values . . . more meaningful values. Don't you think that's so?"

"We are born pure," he said, frowning. "And then the world corrupts us. The only honest thing is what you call primitive. Sensation. The beauty and innocence of it. Love, I mean. Love power."

"It's not innocent to take what you want because

141

the surge of sensation demands it," I protested. "Suppose I fell in love with Janet's husband. Suppose I decided he could give me physical pleasure and so I demand that he satisfy my cravings. Is that kosher, would you say?"

"Certainly. There's no tomorrow. We owe ourselves everything we can get."

I laughed in spite of myself. I didn't want to hurt his feelings, but I couldn't help chuckling at his naiveté. "You don't *do* these things," I said, trying to be gentle. "There's a higher law than our own infantile desires. Don't make me sound pompous, Dennis darling."

"I only know we only pass this way once, and whatever we can get we have a right to," he retorted, and his face darkened.

"Okay." I looked out at the water. "That's the way you feel now. It will change. Want to race me to that jetty?"

"No," he said, and moved toward me. I sensed his intention and yet was not prepared for it. I saw his eyes . . . light, brilliant, steel-gray . . . his eyes were purposeful. "Oh no," I said, taking a step backward, but it was too late. I was in his arms, and his mouth was on mine. I felt the iron of his hard young leg muscles pressed against mine. The sun was blotted out, and his teeth ground against my teeth . . . and I was at once revolted and sorry for his self assurance, which made it certain for him that his caresses would inflame me. Inflame me they did, but had the opposite result. I had thought him a strange, beautiful boy, but the scent of him, masculine and unwelcome because it was not *his* masculinity I wanted, revolted and sickened me. I would have liked to feel pity for

142

him because he was young and so confident but I felt, instead, disgust.

I wrenched away. "You know, this is the furthest thing from my mind," I said coldly. "There's nothing wrong with my responses and I'm not frigid, my young friend. *But I don't want you.*"

I saw the impact sink in; he stiffened and his steel-gray eyes bored into mine. "I don't want you either," he said. "You're a body, though, and you're not too old . . . and I thought it might give you some thrills. They say old maids want it bad." He put a finger to his forehead. "Just trying to do my good deed for the day."

His words were insufferably rude, but his face was young, hurt and wounded. He looked maimed, like a fallen stag, and in my idiocy and compassion I couldn't stand it. "Oh, Dennis," I said. "I'm sorry. You're very nice, very good-looking. It's just that . . . I don't need you."

Clearly, it was the worst thing I could have said. His face went blank while his eyes hardened. He stood straight and gave me a look of total hatred. "If you ever do," he said, "don't bother to ask. I wouldn't touch you with—"

"That's enough," I said, anger flaring at last. "That's quite enough. If you say another word I shall find it quite inexcusable." I glared at him. "I'm afraid I'll have to tell Mrs. Saxon that I find you bad company for Fleur . . . and Tony. I don't know who you are, but I'm almost sure you're a bad influence here. I—"

"Say something like that and you're dead," he said

143

quietly. "I mean it. Open your mouth and you'll be sorry. You'll regret it."

"You young idiot," I said angrily. "Telling me to watch out for someone like you! Are you out of your mind? Go soak your head. How dare you threaten me!"

I gave him one last look and stalked away. I hated myself for it, but I wanted to put distance between me and this old, young man as quickly as possible. Afraid? Yes, in a surprising, hateful way. Afraid of his arrogance, of his stupid, infantile incomprehension. Who knew what this creature might be capable of?

He didn't come after me. And when I knew I had left him far behind, I looked back. He was small now, way in the distance, his beautiful, delicately-muscled body one with the horizon, like a dark god, like a fallen angel.

Chapter 11

I had been reading, in installments, "The Rime of the Ancient Mariner" to Jan's children. Huddled together on the warm sands, with the surf roaring in our ears, we sat in a semi-circle. There were four of us. Roger, Alex Junior, me, and my doll Olympia.

Olympia, who had become part of every activity in the Saxon household, sat with blank eyes and red, pouty lips, listening, along with the two little boys, to the classic lines of Coleridge. She had a greasy mouth, where the children had force-fed her with cereal at the breakfast table. Her stiff eyelashes were, by now, encrusted with sand. Her clothes had been taken off her long ago; she was naked, with a protuberant belly, but she showed no signs of shame.

I had to laugh at her wanton show of uncovered rubber flesh. With that made-up face, those rouged cheeks . . .

She was propped up against a small rock, listening with unblinking eyes to the lines I was quoting.

"But tell me, tell me! speak again
Thy soft response renewing—
What makes that ship drive on so fast?
What is the ocean doing?"

Roger got up and looked at the sea. He glared at it and, doing a kind of bugaloo, repeated, "What is the ocean doing?"

And then Alex joined him in a kind of tribal dance, both of them chanting.

"What . . . is . . . the ocean . . . doing . . ."

I watched them, amused. They were so sweet, made no sense of Coleridge, but liked his rhythms, his mysterious questions, his phantasmagoria of riddles and conundrums. Finally, throwing down the black-bound book, I got up too, and made myself part of their dance. We held hands and sang together.

What is the ocean doing . . . doing . . . doing . . ."

In the midst of this Gertrude came down and told the boys that it was time for lunch, please to come up and eat and Miss Kip, do you want fish or steak?

I wasn't hungry, and told her so. I said thank you, I'd have a snack later on in the afternoon. And then they left me, all of them climbing up the wooden steps, and I started walking along the beach. The sun went under and then came out again, but there was a mackerel sky, which meant rain ahead.

Even here, I thought, the sunshine must give way to thunder and lightning. And as the sky darkened, ominously, I started retracing my steps.

But it was only a dark cloud, and a minute later brightness shone through again. The rain would not

146

come today. Perhaps not tomorrow, either. I sat down and examined a piece of driftwood, shaped like a human female form, with attenuations that looked like arms and legs and a great, pregnant belly. I should take this back and try to sell it to one of those Third Avenue places, I thought absently, and wondered how it would be if I lived out here and ran one of those shops in a place like Morro Bay, where they sold oddities just such as this.

In fact, my future was very much on my mind. I won't always be twenty-six years old, I reminded myself. I picked up a dry twig and wrote to myself in the sand.

You won't always be twenty-six years old.

Then I scraped out the letters, impatiently, and walked all the way back. From a distance I saw the book, the volume of Coleridge, on the sand, and then . . .

Something else.

How odd, I thought. How odd Olympia looks . . .

I stood still for a minute longer and then I started running.

Tony was the first person I saw when I got to the house. He was on the sundeck, munching on a chicken leg, with a bottle of Dr. Pepper balanced on his lap. "Hi," he said, as I climbed the wooden steps. "Whatcha doin', Kip?"

"Olympia's been murdered," I gasped.

"Wha'?"

He looked at me open-mouthed, still chewing.

"Someone tore my doll apart. It's all in bits and pieces."

147

He got up, looking a little stupid. "What is this?" he asked.

"I'm not kidding, Tony. Olympia's been dismembered."

"You mean . . . the doll?" he asked, looking dazed. There was a kind of unbelieving smirk on his face. "You mean that crazy doll?"

"Someone tore her to pieces."

"What the hell . . ."

"Come and see!"

He wiped his mouth, put down his plate, and set the soft drink bottle on the planks of the deck. "Okay," he said, looking puzzled, and followed me. We went down the long flight of steps, walked across the sand and I showed him.

"Look at that," I said, pointing.

The doll, ripped apart, was scattered over the sand. Arms, legs, dimpled hands. The naked torso was headless, its belly staring at the sun.

The head, with its closed eyes, long-lashed, was several yards from the rest of the scattered remnants. The cupid's bow mouth, red and pouting, was silent. Olympia would never say Mama again.

Tony plopped down to the sand.

"It was only a stupid doll," he said after a while.

But there was stupefaction in his eyes, and his face was grave. We both stared at the dismembered doll silently, and Tony didn't say anything more after that. In a little while he crawled about, picking up the pieces, and dug a hole in the sand. A deep hole.

"Alas," he said. "Poor Yorick, I knew him well."

He said that when he stuffed the doll's skull into the sand.

And soon there was nothing left of Olympia. She was all buried in the sand, without benefit of unction, a dead doll that somebody had torn savagely apart.

Torn to pieces.

The message was clear.

This can happen to you too . . .

"It was Dennis," I said, when Tony stood up.

"Dennis?"

"Yes, of course."

"Yes. Dennis did it."

"But *why?*"

I told him. "His last words still ring in my ears," I said. " '*Say something like that and you're dead.*' He wanted to pay me back. I'm sorry, Tony, I know he's a friend of yours. But there aren't very many children any more, not these days. He was furious at my rejection of him and so he took his revenge. Who else? Fleur? The children? Janet or Alex? Of course it was Dennis."

"Christ," he said. "I just can't believe it."

"Tony, I *know.*"

After a while we trudged back and went up the stairs and I was thinking, how could I tell the children? How could I explain the absence of Olympia? Even the destruction of a doll meant death, and why should children be exposed to death?

Not this early, not this soon.

It was Tony who solved the problem. "You must say that Olympia had to go to the hospital," he told me. "She had to have her tonsils out. Tonsils and adenoids."

And it worked. They were both rather upset, but

149

they credited it. "Oh, poor Olympia," they mourned, but they had Gertrude wash and iron the doll's clothes, so that when she was able to return she would be decently clad.

And then they forgot.

"What happened to the doll?" Janet asked me idly.

I said the fantasy had gone far enough.

And that, substantially, was the end of it.

Until the next morning.

Tony sought me out. "It wasn't Dennis," he said.

"What wasn't Dennis?"

"The doll."

"What do you mean? It *had* to be Dennis!" But I saw at once that he knew something I didn't. "Why do you say it wasn't him?"

"Because he's in L.A."

"In Los Angeles?" I tried to collect my wits. But then—

Tony said, "He left two days ago. Fleur just got a postcard from him. It *had* to be sent two days ago, considering the mails. So it couldn't have been Dennis, Kip."

"Then who was it?" I demanded.

"Yeah, I've been wondering," he muttered.

"I don't understand."

"Me neither."

"*Someone* wanted to give me a nasty surprise."

"Anyway, I thought I'd better tell you right away."

"Yes, of course."

But it was, admittedly, a rude shock. If it hadn't been Dennis who'd smashed up Olympia . . .

Well, then, there was—for what reason I failed to understand—a person or persons unknown who

150

objected to my presence here. So much so, in fact, that whoever it was had gone to great pains to frighten the visitor from New York.

I decided to tell Janet about it.

I went upstairs to her studio. "Yes?" she called, from behind the closed door.

"It's me. Kip."

"Come in, Kip."

She wasn't painting; she was seated at a large desk near the windows. I saw that she was attending to correspondence. There was a pile of envelopes, some already addressed, and another pile of papers, bills and such. Everything was very neat and tidy, including a roll of stamps.

I apologized for interrupting, but said that there was something I thought she ought to know, as it was bothering me very much and perhaps she could shed some light on it.

"It's about Olympia," I said.

And suddenly there was a commotion down below, outside. It was one of the children screaming, and we both rushed to the windows, Janet almost knocking her chair over.

"What the dickens now?" she cried, and we looked down.

Gertrude was kneeling beside little Roger: his brother was wringing his hands, and the smaller child's face was contorted with pain. "Oh, my God," Jan said. "He's cut himself . . ."

We raced down.

"What is it, Gertrude?" Jan asked, dashing out to the sundeck.

"A bee," Gertrude said. "He was stung by a bee."

151

The child's forefinger was red and terribly swollen. "Thank God it wasn't anything worse," Jan said, relieved. "Well, come inside, poor little thing, and we'll fix it up straightaway."

She took him into the house and applied some first aid. And in a very short time the pain stopped, the swelling went down and Roger quit shaking.

"You have to be careful of these things," Jan said. "Both the boys have an acute allergic reaction to insect bites. The doctor gave me this, bless him. It really does the trick."

She soothed the child. "It doesn't hurt now, does it?"

"Not as much. But why did he bite me? I wasn't doing anything to him."

"Because you smell sweet, as a clean little boy should. So he thought you were a flower."

"I was brave," he said. "I'd like a treat."

"You certainly shall have a treat. An ice cream stick. And if you want, I'll read to you."

"Yes, read to us," Alex Junior cried. *The Wind in the Willows.*

"All right. Kip, want to hunt it up? You'll find it easily enough. It's in the small bookshelf right between their beds."

I had no trouble finding it and when I went down they were all three on the glider, with Jan in the middle. She put the book in her lap and opened to where there was a piece of paper stuck in. "This is only the third time we've read this book," she told me. "But it's a great favorite."

I left them sitting there, because they looked so delightful. Portrait of Mother and Children, I thought, and tactfully withdrew. Then I remembered that I had left a cigarette burning in the studio, and went on up.

In her haste, Janet had mussed the pile of letters she'd been working on and, automatically, I started to straighten them out. If you believed in preordination (which I didn't and never had) you could say that it was my destiny to find what I did. I wasn't nosy: I was only trying to restore the former order to Jan's desk, though I must confess that I did look to see if there was a letter addressed to Norma.

There wasn't.

I looked through the pile of addressed envelopes, with the letter, or check, inserted under the flap, prior to being put into the envelope and then sealed. She does everything just like me, I thought, faintly amused. Wrote the letters, then addressed the envelopes, and stuffed them all at once . . . after which she pasted on the stamps.

It was the fact that one check was different from the others that made me look twice at it. The other checks were the usual bilious yellow, with Janet's name and address printed at the top. But one check differed. That check was pale green and much larger, at variance with the rest.

Not curiosity, not yet.

Until I saw the amount for which it was drawn, which was one thousand dollars.

It was a cashier's check, and it was payable to someone by the name of Eugene Berne. I turned over the envelope. Under the name was a box number. X 234, San Francisco, California.

I put it back in its place, crushed out my cigarette, and left the studio.

And then went down to my room.

I wanted to think. To be alone and think. A thousand dollars. To someone whose address was only a box number. That was odd, wasn't it?

Why?

Janet had been paying bills, and one of them had been for a thousand dollars.

But I wasn't easy about it. A thousand dollars, even in these inflated days, was a fair amount of money. How was it Jan was paying bills of that size? Why not her husband? Why not Alex?

But what really threw me was the cashier's check. Why not a regular bank check like the others? There was, of course, a very simple answer, an answer that came easily enough. A cashier's check wouldn't reflect on the stubs of a regular checking account. A cashier's check was, in a way, a secret transaction.

Why should a payment of money be secret?

There were innocuous explanations, though offhand I couldn't think of any, but then I wasn't exactly versed in the ins and outs of high finance. I just thought the whole thing was somewhat irregular. I wrote out a substantial number of checks myself, and couldn't figure out why someone should make a payment with a cashier's check. You wanted your records straight, for taxes *et al.*, and therefore the reflection of a payment on a bank stub was important.

Unless . . .

Unless you didn't want that particular payment to be known. Unless you wanted it hidden, private, obscured from anyone else.

But why would Janet want anything like that?

I got up and went downstairs.

154

There were telephone directories in one of the rooms; I had seen them. And I pulled out the San Francisco directory.

I turned to the "B"s. And found the name Berne. There were not very many Bernes. Perhaps a dozen or so.

There was no Eugene Berne. No Berne with the initial E in front of it.

Whoever Eugene Berne was, he didn't have a listed number.

I decided that I very much wanted to talk to Janet's mother.

Chapter 12

My visit to the Lances was solicited, as it turned out, because the very next morning Jan's mother rang up and asked me over to tea. I spent most of the day at the beach and then, at four o'clock bathed, changed and, in a demure cotton dress and my highest heels, went over.

Caroline Lance showed me through the rooms of the small but charming house. Mr. Lance's pajamas were hung on a hook of a bathroom door . . . an intimacy that embarrassed me, though I couldn't have said why. Except that it was difficult to picture Edward Lance *en deshabille*. Or for that matter, Caroline Lance. They were like persons who were always dressed, with shoes and socks and collars.

But of course they went to bed at night, like everyone else.

Mrs. Lance had a green thumb, and there were glorious plants all over. African violets and begonias, snake plants and ferns, Jerusalem cherries and small, winsome orange trees.

"How beautiful," I kept saying.

"All it takes is love and care," she assured me.

"I do love your house," I said.

"Yes, isn't it precious? We never think of Illinois. And Jan's house. So *unusual*."

I said yes, I loved Jan's unusual house.

"This isn't the cheapest place to retire to," she confided. "I suppose the acreage here is about the highest in the country, but to be near Janet, and the children, is worth every penny."

We joined Mr. Lance in the living room for watercress sandwiches and liver pate on melba toast. The coffee was excellent, and afterwards there was B and B.

And Mr. Lance's view of politics was to the far right, as it had always been. I let him talk and then, when the plates of food were empty, he got up and excused himself.

"You don't mind, there's a ball game on television," he said.

"I don't mind at all."

When he went out Mrs. Lance filled my liqueur glass again and I became very courageous and asked what was wrong with Janet. "Do you have any idea?" I asked, leaning forward.

"With Janet?" she repeated incredulously.

"Yes, I . . ." I cleared my throat. "Don't you feel there's some . . . some problem hanging over her?"

She raised astonished eyebrows. "Why, my dear girl, darling Kip," she said. "Whatever can you *mean?*

Why, Janet is so lucky! So fortunate! An illustrious husband . . . two adorable children . . . a busy, active household."

She laughed merrily. "Wrong with Janet? Why, she's one of the most blessed people I know!"

"Yes, I suppose she has . . . certain compensations."

I looked at Mrs. Lance and pulled in my horns. So she didn't see anything wrong. She thought Janet was lucky . . . happy.

"Why, she has *everything*," Mrs. Lance exclaimed.

"Yet she doesn't seem exactly—" I broke off. Well, after all. Jan's mother was looking at me utterly dumbfounded.

"Doesn't seem exactly what?" she demanded.

"I just thought she seemed a little—"

"Yes?"

I retreated. Her tone was distinctly hostile. Briefly, I hated her, then sagged in defeat. What could I have expected? A shallow, selfish woman, utterly caught up in her own concerns. Mrs. Lance was the last person to sense her daughter's unhappiness. Mrs. Lance was a soft-liver, a narcissist, a parasite. I tried to think of something to cancel my previous sentiments.

"I think maybe Jan's working too hard," I said feebly. "Trying to combine an artist's life with a wife's life."

"Janet is a very fulfilled woman," Mrs. Lance said loudly and firmly. "I'm very pleased about Janet. And I'm fond of Alex. It's wonderful having a musical son-in-law. And those beautiful little boys . . ."

"Yes."

159

She chattered on. "That fabulous house. How reassuring to be away from large cities. One never has to lock doors . . ."

You bitch, I thought, hating myself for my enmity. But she was a selfish, self-centered woman, catered by to a doting husband. She didn't see the forest for the trees. Her daughter was troubled and miserable . . . but Mrs. Lance would never guess that. She was too concerned about her hair and skin care and her plants.

I went home frustrated, flushed and none the wiser. I hadn't learned one single thing from the Lances, and was no further ahead than I had been before.

Dennis was back the next day and, although he was his usual irritating self, bad-mannered and arrogant, I was so apologetic about blaming him for the death of Olympia that I bent over backwards being nice to him.

It was just after twelve, and Tony and I were together on the sundeck. Tony was bolting down a quick lunch as a break from his labors when a sound made me turn. Dennis rounded the bend of the wooden stairs, put both hands on the railing and leapfrogged over the deck.

"Hi, how was the smoggy city?" Tony asked.

"Smoggy. What's that you're drinking?"

"Iced tea."

"Who wants to make me a gin and tonic?"

"No hard liquor served at *this* bar until just before dinner," Tony said.

"Come on, don't be exasperating," Dennis said, dropping into a chair and putting his feet up on the railing. "I need a good stiff drink."

"Sorry as hell," Tony said, grinning. "No booze until six or thereabouts. Missy Janet very firm about that."

"What a draggy pad this is," Dennis said, sulking, but in the end gave up. Gertrude brought him out a glass of iced tea and then Zoltan came out, padding softly on zori sandals that showed his splayed feet.

"Well, *Mr.* Varga," Dennis said insolently. "What *do* you mean taking a break from your major opus? I thought you'd be hard at work on those masterpieces of yours." He raised bright blue, impertinent eyes. "Having a little trouble?"

"Plenty of trouble," Zoltan said imperturbably. "I go to bed and it's all there, in my mind, it flows. I have everything written in those wakeful hours between midnight and dawn. But of course as soon as I get up it has slid away from me, like mercury zigging off in all directions. Writing," he said succinctly, "is hell."

"Is that a fact?"

"Then why do you do it? If it's such hell? Why do you waste your time?"

"What's not a waste of time?" Zoltan asked, apparently not at all offended. "What *is* worthwhile?"

"Feeling," the boy said flatly. "Being. Smelling, tasting, *living*. Anything else is an escape."

"I see. Fancy it! So many creative people wasting their time . . ."

"Yes, plenty of them," Dennis said disagreeably. "Wasting hours, days, months, years."

"What's your recipe?" Zoltan asked interestedly. "I mean, your solution for a modus vivendi?"

The boy's light eyes, against the bronzed face,

161

blazed. His eyes seemed blind, almost. They were so blue, so azure. "We live differently," he said stridently, his voice hard-edged. "We refuse to live your way. It's as simple as that."

"Who's we?" Zoltan asked.

"Us," Dennis said. "All of us. My friends. Fleur. Tony. All of us."

"Not me," Tony said. "I don't live the way you say. I work hard. I work very hard."

"At any rate," Zoltan said, "you've named only three people. Just you three? You and Fleur and Tony?"

"Not me," Tony cried. "I work hard!"

And Dennis, goaded, said, "Anyway, all of us. Youth! The youth of this country, of the world. We don't want your rotten world; we intend to make our own."

"Just so you keep the trains running," Zoltan said mildly. "But I still don't understand you. You say youth. Are you young?"

Dennis blinked, and for a moment he looked a little stupid. Then he recovered himself and said, "I'm seventeen. That's young, isn't it?"

"But you lie," Zoltan said. "You lie."

This time the boy flushed. "Would you like to see my birth certificate, Mr. Varga?"

"Your birth certificate has nothing to do with it. It's valueless. As a matter of fact, Dennis, I'll tell you how old you are. You're sixty-two."

This rendered Dennis speechless for a few seconds, and then he burst out laughing. His white teeth flashed in a derisive smirk. "And how do you arrive at that conclusion?" he asked insolently.

"Easy. You're sixty-two. You're also five. And twenty-six, like Kip here. And you're thirty, going on forty. For all I know, you may be ninety."

The boy's face was dark and sullen. "Would you care to elucidate?" he demanded, with stilted sarcasm.

"Sure. But in your deepest soul I believe you know what I mean. This isn't a war between the old and the young, for the young are old and the old are young, and the generation gap is in our favor, those you call the old. Because we can remember, compare, and evaluate far more than you can. You, who are chronologically only seventeen years old, have a poverty of experience compared to me, at fifty-seven. And I must tell you, Dennis, that I am seventeen just as truly as you are. And I am also three and am also seventy and am also forty . . . and we can carry this as far as you wish. Except that it is *not* what you wish. You wish to be seventeen. Or twenty. Or twenty-five. But beyond that you do not wish. Because then you will be dying more rapidly and you will have to confront the truth which will be slowly dawning on you . . . unwilling, frightened, unbelieving. You are all Peter Pans, your wistful, touching generation, idealistic in theory and shockingly naive as to the meaning of existence. All creatures are born to die, to get old, to get ugly, to survive at the expense of others . . . for survival is the ultimate reality. And even you, who claim to be seventeen years old, are already a failure, for you are doomed, were doomed from the moment you left the womb and drew breath. Doomed to die . . . and because survival is the meat and meaning of life, it follows inexorably that the failure to survive, namely to

163

die, is the preordained tragedy that awaits you, awaits us all."

The young boy, no match for Zoltan's polemics, lashed out angrily, flushed and furious. "Meanwhile," he said loudly, "we know how to live. You made the wars: we'll unmake them. You stab in the back to get the job someone else deserves better. You dress clean and neat, and underneath you're sleeping with your best friend's wife. You—"

"I don't sleep with Mrs. Saxon," Zoltan said mildly. "I doubt she'd permit it. Besides, the fire has been out for quite a long time. And it never was my inclination to seduce the wives of my best friends."

"You and your middle class morality," Dennis said, flailing wildly now. He wanted to draw blood any way he could, and so he added, viciously, "You were a dud from the day you were born, Zoltan. You're a has-been and a washout." He rushed on. "We'll remake the world. We'll wipe out greed, and sentimentality and—"

"Good for you, good for you," Zoltan said. "And while you're about it, can you manage to stop the inflation spiral? Because that would be a big load off my mind. I also plead with you to do a little something about crime on the streets, which I understand from all published statistics is limited almost exclusively to persons under twenty. If you can do that, I'm for your militant generation, Dennis."

The boy's cruel jibes had not gone unfelt; I knew from what Zoltan said next that they had cut deep, been keenly registered. "And you must promise me one thing, while we're on the subject. When you have reached the age of maturity—and reason—will you

164

stop and remember what it was like to be seventeen? With all those shining resolutions? Because if you can do that, and if millions of you can do that, another war might be prevented. A war *you* can make, if you forget." He paused, and then said again, almost in a whisper, "if you forget."

"We'll never make a war," Dennis shouted. "Under us, there will never be a war."

"Ah," Zoltan said, and it was almost a sigh. "*Under* you. Oh, Dennis, that word under." There was a flash from Zoltan's eyes that was almost light lightning. "*Under,* you said. *Under* is a terrible word. A frightening word. Well, then, will history repeat itself?"

He looked long at Dennis, and shook his head. Then he shrugged. "But of course," he said, almost absent-mindedly. "It's your world now. You're welcome to it. Take it; I bequeath it to you. For me, it's a lost world."

His eyes brightened suddenly. "But just the same, I am still seventeen, beautiful young boy, and no one can take that away from me. I am seventeen, and the chestnut trees bloom in the Champs Elysees . . . and I am in love." His head went up proudly. "It's mine," he said softly. "It belongs to me, it's in my brain, my experience. Rule the world, then, storm trooper. It makes no difference to me . . . not any more."

There was a silence. I had to credit Dennis with some sensitivity at least. What Zoltan had said had made an impression . . . dimly, perhaps, but the boy, who was not really stupid, knew that this scholar, this disciple of the philosophers, had bested him. He sat

165

defeated, angry, befuddled and frustrated . . . but defeated.

He made only one last try. "You can talk up a storm," he said sulkily. "But can you put me down physically?"

"Name your weapons," Zoltan said.

"The Indian strong-arm," Dennis retorted defiantly. "Let's see which one of us breaks first."

"You mean this?" Zoltan asked, and grasped the boy's wrist.

"Yeah."

"Okay. One, two, three," Zoltan said challengingly, and both pitted their strength against each other.

I watched, embarrassed and angry. I hated to see Zoltan defeated on purely physical terms. They struggled, with Dennis glaring at his opponent.

And then, unbelievingly, I saw Dennis give slightly, saw things going Zoltan's way. I could scarcely credit it, but Dennis was losing. There was a dull flush on his cheekbones as he realized that here too Zoltan was going to win.

"You put up a good fight," Zoltan said, as he brought Dennis' arm to the level of the table. He wore the laurel wreath of victory modestly. "Next time you might make a fool of me, Dennis. You have damned good muscle control."

There was, for a few seconds, a hostile silence. I found myself feeling terribly sorry for Dennis. He had been flayed verbally and then beaten with pure brute strength. I hadn't imagined that Zoltan possessed that kind of physical mastery.

At the moment I didn't know whose side I was on. I admired Zoltan, esteemed his good mind and all of his unusual qualities. Just the same, if you bled for the underdog, you were bound to feel pity for those bested.

And besides, Dennis hadn't killed Olympia.

Somebody else had.

Chapter 13

Oddly enough, I met Dennis' mother the very next day. It was odd because his mother turned out to be someone I had heard spoken about; that she was *who* she was came as something of a surprise.

Alex and I were having breakfast on the sundeck, with the children. "Stop that," Alex said when Roger bubbled his milk.

"It's fun to do."

"I don't care if it's fun. Don't do it."

I had been at Xanadu for just under two weeks. And in all that time Janet had only sat down to a morning meal with us, so far as I could recall, two or three times. Wasn't that a strange thing, I was thinking and then, as we were having our second cup of coffee Dennis clumped up the stairs, two at a time from the sound of it and sat down to the round table. He said a brief hello and started reaching for things; the coffee pot, Gertrude's home-made coffee cake. He finished a piece and cut himself a second.

And then, palming a cube of sugar into his mouth, he went away with an off-hand, "Thanks, see you."

I'll never warm to Dennis, I thought.

"What's the matter?" Alex asked, seeing my lofty expression.

"Nothing. Except that I wish someone would teach that boy manners."

"Well, he's not very well-adjusted. Nor is he fortunate in his background."

I didn't say anything. Other children had broken homes. And somehow they managed to survive and make a life. Why was Dennis so special?

"I think we can give him the benefit of the doubt," Alex said mildly.

"But what puts me off about him is that he's mad at the world. An attitude like that isn't going to help him win friends and influence people. As a matter of fact, Alex, I *am* trying to lean over backwards. I've a particular reason for wanting to be nice to him."

"What's the particular reason?"

"I thought he was guilty of . . . of something he wasn't guilty of."

"What?"

"Just something," I said. "It's not important."

"I'd like you to meet his mother," Alex said.

"Is that really necessary?"

He hid a smile. And then lit a cigarette.

"No, not necessary," he said, exhaling smoke. "But I have a feeling you'll like her. And that she'll like you. Let's make a date. I'll call her and say we'll drop in on her around five this afternoon. I'll meet you here at a little before, and we'll walk over. It's just down the beach a way."

As we trudged across the sand, later that afternoon, I asked Alex about what work he might have in progress.

"If any," I said. "You have such a busy life it's hard to see how you can compose at the same time."

"The more you do the more you *can* do," he said. "Energy begets energy. And yes, I do have a work in progress. It's an opera, based on *The Aspern Papers* by Henry James, laid in Venice. I've had it in my mind for a long time. I'm quite keen on the project."

"It sounds fascinating," I said. "How far have you gone?"

"I've done two acts, roughly, of course. The third act is difficult. I'm sweating over it."

"I wish you luck."

"Thanks. And here we are."

He went ahead of me, climbing up a path that loomed suddenly. And in a second or two a very pretty cottage, in a clearing, became visible. There was an open door, and Alex called out.

"Hi, Mimi?"

Mimi.

I looked quickly at him. And remembered Lola Montray saying: *"My friend Mimi . . . if a man's wife left the scene, and he turned to you . . ."*

So Lola Montray's friend Mimi was Dennis' mother.

Without waiting for an answer Alex stood aside for me to enter, and then followed me in. And in a second or two, as we walked through a kitchen area, someone called out, "Hello, is it you, Alex?"

"Yes, it's both of us," he called back.

And then we were in a large, comfortable, cluttered room which, like Jan's studio, was stacked with can-

171

vases, an easel, tables where jars of brushes swam in colored water, and a great sweep of windowed wall that gave us a view of the sunset.

The woman that came up to us held out a hand to me and, still gripping mine, leaned past me and planted a kiss on Alex' cheek. "Gee, I'm glad you popped over," she said. "I was feeling lonely today."

She was a gorgeous, overblown, dark-haired, violet-eyed woman in her late thirties. She was in a smock the color of her eyes, open at the throat, and revealing a deep cleavage. She was heavily-tanned, without make-up and needing none. She had a full, ripe, almost voracious mouth.

She wore gold hoop earrings that swayed as she moved about.

"What's everyone drinking?" she asked.

Her voice was low-pitched and faintly husky, with a laugh in back of it.

"Could I have scotch?" Alex asked.

"Of course you can have scotch. I've never known you to drink anything but scotch."

"Me too, if I may," I said.

"Two scotches coming up. Water, rocks, or soda?"

"Just rocks," Alex said, and I asked for the same.

While she was making the drinks, and the ice cubes were tinkling, I got up and started looking at canvases. "That's right, mosey about," my hostess said. "I understand you're an artist too."

"Yes."

Her work was good, strong and hard, like a man's work. On one wall hung a magnificent portrait of her son. I thought it was one of the finest of its kind I had ever seen and told her so.

"Well, he's a superb subject," she said. "Don't you think?"

"Yes, he's wonderful looking. Roger thinks he looks like Jesus."

She looked up and laughed. "Oh, how fabulous," she cried. "Jesus! An Aryan Jesus, that's for sure."

She handed me my drink and walked in back of me as I cruised through her studio. Alex sat, his feet up on a hassock, watching us. I was enjoying myself. It was a familiar ambience and a familiar smell . . . paint, turps, the clean, fresh smell of canvas. And after I made a thorough inspection of her work, I sat down beside Alex, and Mimi plumped up a scarlet cushion and, leaning against a parson table, looked up at us. "It's so nice to have company," she said. "Is anyone ready for another drink?"

"Sit," Alex said, looking *so* relaxed, and I had scarcely touched my own drink. We had an awfully nice talk. About everything, it seemed. Children, and divorces, and the way things were these days. The sun sank and the studio grew dark, but no one wanted light. We communed in the semi-dark, and Alex had been right. I felt Dennis' mother liked me. And I *knew* I liked her.

I saw Alex finally look at his wrist, and then he said it was time to go, that the folks at home would be wondering. I saw something else too. The resigned, disappointed look on the face of our hostess. But she scrambled up, said she was sorry it had to end so soon but that she understood.

"There's nothing worse than a burnt meat loaf," she murmured. And then turned to me. "Kip, come on over tomorrow, can't you? Just you yourself? We'll

173

compare notes about our work. I'd like it very much. I mean, darling, if you can spare the time."

"Time is something I have a plethora of at the moment," I said, smiling. "Thank you, Mimi, I'd love to."

"Why do you call me Mimi?" she asked.

It was a totally unexpected question. Why did I call her Mimi? "But isn't that your name?" I asked. "I heard Alex call you that."

"Yes, he calls me that," she said gravely. "I'm used to it from him. But my name is Miriam. It's a good Biblical name. I happen to like it. I'd prefer it if you'd . . ."

Suddenly she laughed that rich, careless laugh again. "Hell, call me anything you want," she said. "What the hell does it matter?"

"Of course it matters," I said. "If you'll promise to call me Katherine, instead of Kip, I'll call you Miriam."

"So you do understand," she said, and there was a queer moment, as we faced each other, two women . . . and for the moment we had forgotten about the man, Alex.

"Yes," I said. "I'm almost sure I do."

"I was almost sure you would," she said in a very soft voice. And then, as she showed us out, she was the glad-hander again, smacking us on the shoulders as we left, and reminding me that I had promised to drop in tomorrow.

"Come around eleven or so," she said. "By that time I'll have waked up enough to be fairly civilized when you get here."

Alex and I walked back. The sand was violet now, and cool, and night was only a short time away. "I think she's a very fine person," I said to Alex. "Thank you for introducing me to her."

"I was *almost* sure you'd feel that way," he said. "Yes, she's . . . superlative. One couldn't have a better friend. I *know*."

He did the usual, found a blade of sand grass and started splitting it. And then, discarding that, found another.

"There was a point in my life," he said, "when I wasn't sure what was going to happen . . . to my marriage. I suppose all first years are difficult; at least the psychologists tell you so. Anyway, except for Gertrude and Tom, Mimi was the only real friend I had."

"I'm sure she was a good friend."

"Oh . . ." He shrugged. "A good friend? None better I don't know what I would have done . . ."

He threw down the second blade of grass almost angrily. "Without her," he said. "And all the time she was having her own gethsemane. A little boy, and an absentee husband . . ."

"Don't talk about it if you don't want to," I said quickly.

He looked at me, considered, and then talked about it. "You see, Janet and I had been married for only a few months. I went to Europe to conduct and at the last minute Janet said she couldn't come with me. She had been seeing a doctor, and his verdict was that she was anemic, seriously so. Therefore, I went alone. It was an extended tour . . . London, Frankfort, Munich, Berlin. Ending up at the Salzburg Festival. Of course all that time I was terribly worried about Jan."

"Yes, of course."

There was a long silence and then he said, in a way that wrung my heart, "I had thought it would be our honeymoon, you see."

"Alex, I'm so sorry it turned out that way."

"Yes," he said. "Yes."

And as I was about to voice another soporific, he said, "I knew it was touch and go then. I was away for seven months. It took a lot out of me, but I was younger then, and I knew I had to solidify my future. And it was a big step toward that."

We walked along silently for a while and then he said, knocking me for a loop, "When I came back Janet was gone."

"Gone?" I looked up at him, astonished. "Gone where?"

"I don't know," he said. "I never did know. I contacted her parents in Illinois. They were as disturbed as I was."

"But what *happened?*"

"I don't know. I probably never will know," he said. "But Janet did come back, as you see. And we had good years together. And then the children . . ."

He watched the water curl up around our feet. It swept toward us, retreated, surged up again and then pulled back, foaming and splashing. The colors of the surface foam were resplendent, taking on the blue of the sky.

"But Mimi," he said quietly. "She gave me such comfort. Understanding. I was selfish, yes, I know. I took what she had to give, gave nothing in return. She was . . . very good to me. Without her, I would have gone under."

He looked at me. "You see, that's why Dennis is like one of the family. Because she was so good to me. I'd do almost anything for that boy, because he's *her* boy. I know his hangups. And maybe he's not even very nice. I'm not sure. I'm not . . . fond of him Not really. But I want to help him."

"I'm not fond of him either," I said honestly. "But knowing the circumstances, meeting his mother, whom I liked very much, I'll try to feel differently about him now."

"I hope so," Alex said.

A chopper burped overhead. It trailed a commercial banner, which streamed against the white-clouded, blue sky.

ADOPT A CHILD, it read, and Alex explained that the philanthropic societies on the West Coast were underwriting a drive for desolate and unwanted orphans. "There are so many of them," he said. "It's a good cause."

"Yes, it's a wonderful cause," I said.

"How terrible for a child to be unloved," Alex murmured.

Next day I made my way across the sands to Miriam Sellaby's cottage. When Alex had introduced us the previous day before it had sounded like Selby, but when I said I had never known Dennis' last name was Selby, she corrected me and spelled it.

"S-e-l-l-a-b-y. Of course it's a simplification. It's a Czech name, originally with a lot of double consonants, cz's and so forth."

177

This morning she said, "Come into my house," and we walked back, through a none too tidy kitchen, to her studio.

"I'm giving you Quiche Lorraine for lunch," she announced. "It'll probably be horrible, I'm a lousy cook, but it won't kill you. At least I don't think it will."

She sat me down.

"But first we drink," she said. "I'm swigging Calvados. Do you want scotch? Or would you care to join me in my decadence?"

I knew Calvados, had drunk it in the south of France, in the Basque regions. Yes, it had a kick, could send you under the nearest table. But I decided I could handle it and said yes, I'd opt for Calvados.

"Good girl," she said, and filled a glass for me. "And now I want to hear about *your* work," she said briskly. "Are you good?"

"I hope so. I think I'm showing a slow, steady improvement."

"Exhibited?"

"A few times."

"No use in asking where," she said, smiling. "I don't know the New York galleries, except for the very big ones, the museums, in fact."

"Not there yet," I said, smiling back. "Maybe some day. Yes, that would be exciting. But for now, in some rather good, smaller galleries."

The bottle of Calvados went down, and it was all very companionable. I liked women, had always liked them. I'd never really known my father; that is to say he died before he was anything but a parent to me. And our house had been filled with young girls.

I was used to women, and I trusted them. Not that

178

men hadn't been decent to me but I knew and was comfortable with my own sex.

"Can I see some more of your stuff?" I asked and she was not averse to displaying it; we went through stack after stack of canvases. And then, astonishingly, there was a portrait of Janet's husband.

She saw my quick, wide-eyed look and pulled it out.

"Do you like it?" she asked, picking it up and propping it against a table.

It was a younger Alex, but that sensitive mouth, dark eyes and soft, thick hair was substantially the same. Those features, at least, hadn't changed. I thought, so that's how he looked when he was *really* young.

"This was done in the late nineteen-fifties," Miriam said matter of factly. "When you were only a tadpole."

"Not quite," I said. "In the late nineteen-fifties I was in my teens."

"Just a baby. Years younger than my son, whom I consider a little boy."

She looked at the portrait, put a finger to her full mouth and then said, "He's quite a man, isn't he?"

"Yes, I like him very much."

"Are you in love with him?"

Her question took me completely by surprise, shocked me.

"No, certainly not," I said.

"Why aren't you?"

"Because—"

"Because he's married to Janet?"

"Because I'm not in love with him. The idea never crossed my mind."

"Then you're a very unusual woman," she said.

179

"The idea would cross almost any woman's mind."

"Not mine."

"*I'm* in love with him," she said.

"Oh."

"Not that it does me any good."

I was silent.

She laughed, a hand on the portrait. "All right, I made a big try and it netted me nothing."

What could I say? What *was* there to say? But I was piecing things together. Alex's telling me about the first year of his marriage, when Janet hadn't gone on that concert tour with him. And then his saying that Miriam had helped him over that crisis.

Lola Montray's words came back to me.

"So she swallowed her bitterness . . ."

Oh, I thought. So it had been like that. And all the time I had been growing up, starting my career and thinking of Janet as someone to whom life had been kind and generous . . .

But there had been strange things in that life. I saw that now.

And there were still strange things.

It would have been better to keep the memory intact, I thought sadly.

"In spite of everything he still loves her," my hostess said abstractedly.

She put the portrait of Alex away, hid it behind other canvases, and poured out some more Calvados.

"But why shouldn't he be in love with her?" I asked.

She looked at me with an equable smile. "Yes, why shouldn't he?" She stretched, showing the outline of her rich, ripe breasts under the loose smock.

There was a rather uncomfortable silence and then

she said, "I like you, Kip. I mean forgive me, Katherine."

I started to say that I liked her too, which I did, but before I could she blurted it out. As if she couldn't help herself.

"I don't like Janet, though."

I was of course put off and couldn't think of anything to say to this admission. She saw my uneasiness and laughed. "Yet I admire her," she confessed. "She's a stunning woman and she has talent. I can admire her and not like her, can't I?"

"Yes, it's entirely up to you how you feel about her," I said.

"Then why do I like you?" she asked.

"I don't know."

"I'll tell you why, and in your heart you know why. I like you because you're warm and human and you're not an enigma. I never did go for the Mona Lisas of this world. They throw me. I'm open, and I like open people. I do what I want to do. Or, let me amend that. I do what I *have* to do. And I survive. I'm a little bit fed up with women who find a haven and cling to it . . . no matter what."

She drank, and put down her glass after filling it again.

"All right, I sound bitchy," she said. "Maybe I am. But—"

"We're all bitchy at times," I said.

"If we weren't, we'd be saints. And do you cotton to saints? I never did."

"I agree. And it doesn't matter how you feel about . . . about anyone else. I *do* like you, and I told Alex so."

181

"And what did Alex say?"

"He said he'd known I would."

"Isn't he nice?"

"Anyway, for some reason I feel I can talk to you and . . . trust you."

"Trust me? About what?"

"Janet," I said.

She burst into laughter. "Couldn't it be something else?"

"All right, then, it's about Alex."

Her smile widened. "Foxy, aren't you? Very well, then, it's about Alex, in connection with Janet."

"In a way."

"Loosen up," she said, looking at me over the rim of her glass, with her violet eyes. "I didn't mean to hurt your feelings. Obviously you're fixated on Janet. So what can I tell you? What is it you want to know?"

"Alex said there was a point in their lives when . . . when you were the only person who helped him."

She shrugged. "Did he tell you that?"

"Yes, but that's all, except that it was at a time when he and Janet were . . . oh, at odds, somehow. He was in Europe conducting and when he came back she had gone."

"Um hum."

She nodded, waiting. She wasn't going to make it easy for me, I saw. For a moment I thought of backing down, and then she smiled and put down her glass.

"That was a long time ago," she said.

She was quiet for a while. And then she leaned her head back against the seat of the couch and spread her hands in a resigned gesture. They were very pretty hands, long and slim, with oval nails.

182

"Yes, there was a crisis and yes, Alex did lean on me. How many times did I talk to him, talk, talk . . . and always hoping Janet wouldn't come back, or he'd have *had* it with her. They'd only been married for a short time. I thought, well, okay, it's gone pffft . . . and of course he was here so much and I had every reason to believe—"

She laughed softly. "That's what women always think. That they have every reason to believe they'll take someone else's place."

She sat up again.

"But . . . uh . . . well, that's because women have a way of kidding themselves. We were born to take a back seat . . . you find that out after a while."

She sipped her drink reflectively.

"Oh, don't think Alex stopped visiting me. You know, talking his heart out, and . . . but never once did he . . . well, let's skip that. 'She's pregnant,' he finally told me, looking as if he'd struck oil in Oklahoma. And so there was baby makes three in due time, and then another baby, and that, my dear, was that."

Her face was controlled and almost cheerful. "And so they lived happily every after," she said, pouring some more Calvados in my glass and then into her own.

"But they didn't," I said abstractedly, and then realized my own betrayal. Her eyes sharpened. "What d'you mean?" she demanded, putting the bottle down with a little bang.

My face must have mirrored my distress.

"Don't worry," she said quietly. "I assure you, don't ever be afraid that . . . in confidence . . . I trust you, you trust me . . . come, what is it you mean?"

183

And recklessly, I told her. Told her about Alex's visit in New York, about his concern for Janet, himself, and their family. And *almost* about the man in San Francisco. But reason intervened, and I didn't say anything about that.

She listened, and the smoke from her cigarette curled up. When I had finished my story we were quiet for a while, not saying anything. She just sat and looked at her hands and I began, in the long, uneasy silence, to feel like Judas.

I shouldn't have said all that, I thought. Why had I said all that?

Then she crushed out a cigarette and looked up.

"Well, I see my role of confidante and good egg is over," she said. "It seems to be your turn now."

She laughed. It had a forced sound, and her smile was twisted. "You see, it all sounds so familiar. This warped worry about Janet. And now he's found someone else to communicate with."

"Oh, but it isn't that! It's not—"

She interrupted me. "I don't like women like her," she said tightly. "Women who use men. Not that I think men are so special. But there's something totally *unfair* about some women . . . that they're adored, worshipped. And—"

"I don't believe it's exactly *that*," I said carefully. "I think he feels responsible for Janet. I'm sure he loves her, perhaps in the wrong way, but . . ."

And then, because her face was so wounded, so desolate, I gave her a little present. Afterwards I asked myself how I could have brought myself to betray my friend that way.

But I did.

"You see, their lives are rather strange," I told her. "I don't know what each thinks about the other. But they're not lovers. At least I don't think so. They have separate rooms, and—"

Her face lightened with a desperate interest. "That doesn't mean anything," she said.

"No. It's more . . . an impression. I feel that was over a long time ago."

I walked back, after lunch, to Xanadu.

The Quiche Lorraine had been creditable, a little watery, but with a very good flavor. She wasn't a bad cook, I thought . . . and she was a very decent woman, a good woman.

I felt . . . well, tired. Sad, puzzled. There was a mystery here in Big Sur. One person knew part of the truth and another person another part. But nobody except Janet knew the whole truth.

The answer lay in Janet.

Chapter 14

It was the day after my second visit to Miriam Sellaby's that Jan started painting me.

"Remember I spoke about the resemblance between us?" she said. "I want to do something that will be you and me, like a split personality. I'm going to emphasize the mutual likeness. It may turn out to be a self portrait. Let's see if I can turn you into me . . . or me into you."

"But there's no real resemblance between us," I insisted.

"You don't see it. I do."

She dressed me up in a dinner dress of hers, a fan-pleated, turquoise-colored Fortuny silk gown. It made me look like a mermaid, clinging to the lines of my body and ending, at my toes, in a kind of filmy froth.

Fortuny gowns had been a rage in the Thirties and Forties; Janet had gotten hers at a San Francisco thrift shop. She took it out of a carton no larger than a wig box; it was meant to be stored that way, all curled up

187

like a snake, and its pleats, as narrow as needle pricks, never lost their sharpness providing it was thus folded and stored.

I had heard about the Fortuny vogue, and that there was a return of it among rich and fashionable matrons of these times, but I had never seen one. I fell in love with it, and to be encased in its silken, swathing folds was like being wrapped in gossamer.

Janet started sketching. "It'll take only a day or two to get the general impression," she told me. "So be patient, okay? I know it's a bore, but I have a feeling this will be a good piece of work."

She was silent and so was I, until it was time to rest. Then she threw down her conte crayon. "Take five," she said. "Goodness, you look like Titania in that shimmering, clinging thing. Come here, Kip."

She led me to the full length mirror on one wall.

"Take a look," she said. "In some odd way, don't we look a bit alike?"

We were the same height. Bony, both of us, with hair that grew the same on the forehead. I *felt*, suddenly, like Janet, in *her* dress, felt that I had left my own identity behind and had assumed hers.

But Janet was beautiful. I had never thought of myself as beautiful.

"Later," she said, "I'll paint in a breaking surf foaming around your feet. Very Botticelli. With a Dali touch. Oh, Kip, you're so young, so heartbreakingly young."

And when I was posing again, she repeated that.

"Kip, you're so young . . ."

She plied her crayon.

"And I'm old."

"How idiotic," I said, laughing. "You're in your mid thirties. For heaven's sake, Jan."

"Late thirties," she said. "But years don't always matter. Some of us die earlier than others. That's one of the great mysteries of life. Some go early, some break."

"But why?"

"Because life is exactly that way," she said absently. "Surely you must realize that."

"Yes, I do, but how . . . why . . . should it apply to you? You have everything going for you. Everything."

"Is that a fact," she said, absorbed in her work.

"Janet—"

"Do you mind," she asked, poising her crayon. "You've moved a bit to the side, Kip. Turn slightly to the right. That's it. Hold it, please."

Two days later she was ready to paint in past the outlines, and let me see the crayon sketch. I was astonished, because it wasn't me at all. It was Janet . . . it *was* a self portrait.

We both worked hard for the next few days. I mean, standing for hours in the same position is *work,* and I felt I earned the late afternoon hours, when we got in Jan's car for a short drive, so that we could get the kinks out of us. We knocked off early one day and went to St. Simeon, the Hearst castle which, in spite of its abominable taste was fantastic in its size and lavishness.

Mostly, we drove hither and yon, not far but giving me a good taste of the environs. I thought this part of California very beautiful, and it reminded me of the novels of Robert Nathan. It had, in some strange way, an unreality that to my disciplined New England mind smacked of forbidden beauty. I told Janet that it was a nice place to visit but that I wouldn't want to live there, and she said she understood what I meant.

"I sometimes feel in the midst of a dream," she confessed and quoted a quatrain from Baudelaire.

> That marvelous landscape of my dream
> Which no eye knows, nor ever will
> At moments, wide awake, I seem
> To grasp, and it excites me still . . .

That was my old, mystical Janet, spouting poetry the way she used to. We were very close for those few days, very close. I knew that I would never feel the same about any other woman. Norma was dear and funny and scintillating, but Janet was unique in my life. I had, and never tried to hide it from myself, an unabashed admiration for her, a kind of love that was whole unto itself. It was a dedication that comes only to the very young, and from which one never recovers.

One day in her studio I almost got to her, almost reached the heart of her problems. "I can't get over how much you are like me," she said, pausing in her work. "You're almost a double."

"Janet, we're totally different types," I protested. "I'm flattered, but—"

"No no, I'm right," she insisted. "You're good, you're good, Kip. It sounds as if I was blowing my own horn, comparing myself to someone like that. But whatever I am I know I'm not unkind, or selfish or cruel. Kip, try not to be hurt, as I was hurt. I pray you won't be, but people like us are so easily taken advantage of."

"Were you hurt, then?" I asked quickly.

"Of course."

"How? How were you hurt, Janet?"

I was excited, almost unbearably so. I felt I was near the truth. Now she would tell me everything . . . and I would know all the answers about Janet.

And then I could begin to help.

A sudden, violent clap of thunder boomed . . . and then the lightning flashed, yellowing the sky. And with that burst of sound Janet's face changed. Deceit stole over it, and protectiveness. Her face, turned to me, became blank, anonymous, and I knew that the accident of the sudden storm coming up, the bolt of lightning and the thunderclap, had spoiled my chances.

She regarded me for a moment more, then got up and went to the window.

"You see?" she said. "It isn't all sweetness and light on this Arcadian coast. We have the vicious elements here too." Her voice became preoccupied. "This looks like a bad one. I must round up the children."

The next morning's painting ended about noon and I went down to my room to get out of my mermaid dress. On the way I ran into Tony coming out of his room and he rushed over and hugged me.

"I did it," he crowed. "I licked that damned, foul son-of-a-bitch problem in scoring. It's been bugging me for over a week! Only a genius could have done what I did. Shake hands with a genius, Kip."

I shook hands with him.

"And now," he said, "how about a fun afternoon?

Let's drive to Sausalito. Let's have ourselves a time."

"Sure, I'll tell Janet," I said.

But Janet begged off. "I know Sausalito like the back of my hand," she said. "Include me out, except thanks anyway."

"Oh, can't you come?" I begged.

"Darling, it would only be a drag for me," she said. "Forgive me, do."

I hunted up Tony again, said I'd join him as soon as I changed into a proper dress and, in fifteen minutes, searched for him . . . he was on the sundeck, talking to Zoltan.

"I'm trying to get this guy to come with us," he said.

"Yes, come with us, Zoltan."

"But I have work to do," Zoltan explained.

"Let it go for one day, for Jiminy sake," Tony coaxed. "You may never meet a genius again." He was very persuasive. "I have a whole day planned out. We'll make the Sausalito scene and then go to Chinatown and have dinner at Kan's, about eight or so. It'll be a swell day, the three of us."

"Yes, please," I said. "I want to go to Ghiradelli Square, and I need your moral support."

"You want to go *where?*" he asked.

"All right, you've forgotten. But I told you, only you've forgotten. That man who was snapping pictures that day. Of Jan's children."

"But what—"

"I know the house. I want to take a look inside. Maybe I can—"

"But Kip, you're overcompensating," he said, chidingly.

"Just the same, I intend to do it. So come with us. Please. I'll feel so much better."

He shook his head unhappily, said we were both young idiots but in the end agreed to come with us. "Wait for me in the car," he instructed. "I won't be long. Just something I have to do."

Tony and I sat in the car, the Mustang, playing a game we both liked, a rather primitive game but a time-killer. Making big words into little ones. Tony picked the word "strangers," and I started taking it apart.

There were lots of words: *strange, angers, grants, rants, rents, tears, rest* . . . and so on.

Tony was counting on his fingers.

"That's seven," he said. "Come on, I can think of at least three more."

And then Zoltan came out, waddling in his characteristic way toward the car and Tony whispered, "Sometimes I expect him to say quack quack."

"Hang on to your wig, Kip baby," he said to me, when Zoltan had climbed in the back. "We're going to make tracks. Sausalito or bust."

He drove much too fast and we were there in a little under three hours.

And leave it to Tony . . . he found a parking space without even trying. A car pulled out of a space and Tony slid in. "It's a gift," he said modestly, when I commented on his luck. "You either have it or you don't."

Sausalito was very attractive, clambering up the sides of a hilly terrain and it reminded me of Naples, or Amalfi, with its sea view, its sun-bleached houses and its simplicity. It was arty in some places, with only a few modern apartment buildings marring its quiet charm. The Glad Hand, a restaurant with no pretensions at all, cluttered, even junky, but warm and hospitable, was quite fun.

The food was plain but good; we each had a sirloin, rare and bloody, and hearty drinks beforehand. Later, we roved through some interesting shops; stores that sold handsome posters, Villagy jewelry shops and a couple of stores that offered leather goods . . . belts, sandals, handbags and so forth. We ended up with a drink at Sally Stanford's; Tony furnished me with the history of this demi-mondaine lady, who once was the Polly Adler of the Pacific coast, and indeed her establishment resembled a bordello, all red plush and gilt paneling.

"Zak's doesn't exist any more," Tony told me. "Sorry about that. They used to have turtle races there. There are still turtle races in Sausalito on Sundays, but its not the same. Zak's was where it was *at*."

We drove over the bridge and shortly after that were at Ghiradelli Square.

"All right," Tony said. "Here you are, Kip. *Now* what do you want to do?"

"I want to look around," I said. "Leave me off here and pick me up in a quarter of an hour. All right?"

"Do you *have* to do this?" Zoltan asked, frowning, and I said, smiling, "No, but I'm going to just the same."

And then Tony let me off at the corner of Hyde and Bay Streets.

I watched the car drive away and then crossed over to the row houses. The one which Janet's friend had

194

entered was substantially like the others; they were all attached, with a common roof. Each had embellishments stuck arbitrarily on the front facade: the one I was interested in had a festoon of grape leaves graven into the stone, and from top to bottom was bay-windowed. There were sand-colored drapes at the window of the first-floor bay; above that were ivory Venetian blinds, and the third story had wooden shutters half closed. The top floor had nothing at the windows at all.

I went up three stone steps and entered a small vestibule. There was a row of mailboxes, brass and highly burnished. My breathing had quickened; I was very nervous.

I looked at the names on the boxes.

There were only four names. I saw mine right away.

There was an A. Anderson, a Lewis Segal, a Dorothy Murray.

And there was a Howard Dolphs.

Howard Dolphs was 1A.

Howard Dolphs . . . It was an odd name . . . a name that made you think of a dolphin.

So his name was Howard Dolphs, I told myself, and then, with a kind of wild surprise asked myself what I was doing looking at highly-polished mailboxes. Here I was, standing in *this* place! Fools, I thought, rushed in where angels feared to tread.

And yet, inside this small foyer, I knew that now I had taken a first, tentative step. I had seen the full name of Janet's lover, had gone into the entrance of the house where he lived . . . and it was like making everything real. I knew now, irrevocably, that this house was a part of Jan's life. Her feet had covered

195

this ground, perhaps countless times . . . and Janet, after ringing the bell, or using a key, had opened that front door and gone inside, closing the other part of her world behind her.

There were suddenly quick footsteps inside the house, audible from where I stood, and I turned sharply, in a blind panic. The door opened and a man came out.

We gave each other a sidewise glance as he caught up to me in the small foyer. My heart quieted down. It wasn't Howard. It was a very pleasant-looking, bearded young man in his late twenties. He pushed open the outer door and then it slammed behind him.

And then I followed him quickly out.

I was just on the top step when I realized something.

Howard Dolphs' apartment was 1A. That meant that the windows I was passing as I flew down the stone steps were his. I glanced apprehensively toward them and, just as I reached the bottom step I saw a hand.

The hand pulled aside the drapes.

I didn't wait any longer. I wasn't sure whether I had glimpsed a bright, blond head . . . or if I only thought so because of the hand yanking apart the drapes . . . and because—

Because it was *his* apartment.

I was on the point of hysteria. If that had been Howard at the window, then he would know I was spying on him, would tell Janet, "Your friend was here, peering into my windows . . ."

Why had I done it?

But I had, and it was too late now.

196

Tony picked me up; I was waiting impatiently, standing on one foot. "Mission accomplished?" he asked.

"More or less."

"Did you find out anything?" Zoltan asked.

"I don't know."

"What's this all about?" Tony demanded. "Zoltan won't say a word."

"It's a secret between Zoltan and me."

"Are you two pash for each other?"

"Could be," I said, and smiled at Zoltan in the rear view mirror. "Where are we going now?"

"The Top of the Mark. Just for a drink. There's a view like you wouldn't believe. You can go back and tell your friends."

At seven-thirty we were in Chinatown.

It was night now, but not really dark. The lights made, in the fog, catherine wheels, diffused circles of brilliance. The Oriental section of the city was pagodaed and exotic, a conglameration of flimsy structures like *papier mache,* and I spent a lot of money on trinkets in the incense-scented shops. We had dinner at Kan's, then wandered some more, and Tony blew three dollars and bought me a pinky ring in the shape of a serpent. Zoltan, not to be outdone, bought me a snake bracelet which cost a considerable amount more. It was nice to be with two persons of the opposite sex and I felt pampered, spoiled.

I liked it.

Not long afterwards, in spite of a hearty meal, we were nibbling on fried pork out of paper bags. The meat was delicious, succulent and crisp. We were standing at a street corner. The light was red.

"Come on, we can make it," Tony said, and started to hurry me across Grant Street, but our hands were parted as a voluble foursome separated us, and I had completely lost sight of Zoltan. I was left standing at the curb, watching Tony dart across the avenue and looking, over heads, for Zoltan.

Someone jostled against me. I turned at the contact and saw the flash of steel . . . and then heard someone cry out.

Wheeling, ducking, I stifled my own scream, fell face down in the street, my head hanging over the gutter. The dirty pavement was at eye level, filled with street dung, reeking. I saw blood running, and then felt the pain.

It's happened, I thought and stunned, imagined myself back in New York City. It had finally happened . . . the disaster, always vaguely feared, always in the back of my mind, everyone's mind. It had happened to others and now it had happened to me.

I simply lay there, helpless with the sudden horror of it. Then I heard Tony's voice and felt his arms trying to help me up. Stupid with lethargy, resigned, I finally stood, wavering. I was almost unfeeling, but not broken . . . and in spite of my skinned, bleeding chin, was substantially unhurt.

"Are you all right?" Tony asked, his voice high and scared. "Kip, are you all right?"

"I think so."

"What happened?"

Zoltan loomed up, large and reassuring. He put a beefy hand on my arm.

"Someone had a knife," I said.

"*What?*"

They both stared at me, as if I had lost my mind.

I shook my head, trying to clear it. And to assure myself that, of course, I had been mistaken. What kind of crazy things was I thinking? And then heard myself say, "I saw it gleam in the light. I thought it was a knife. I didn't want it to cut me."

I was brushing myself off. I was too dazed to think straight.

Zoltan said, holding me steady, "What do you mean, a knife?"

I said it again. I seemed unable to say anything else. "I think someone lunged at me with a knife." I kept rubbing at my pants and blouse, and I kept repeating the same thing.

"I saw it gleam in the light," I added.

Tony whipped out a hankerchief, held it to my chin and spoke excitedly to the people around us. "Did anyone see what happened?"

The crowd around us melted away, terrified of involvement. We were left standing alone, with Tony stanching the flow of blood from my face. He unleased a stream of invective, but it fell on deaf ears. "They don't care," he said passionately, trying to grab someone. "None of them cares. No one even calls a cop."

"I'm all right," I said. "Please let's go home. I just want to go home."

I was driven back to Xanadu between my two solicitous friends. Tony drove and Zoltan held me against him. "Don't say anything," I said, as we neared the house.

"Why the hell not?" Tony asked.

"Because."

"Because why, damn it?"

"I have my reasons! Don't say anything!"

"I don't dig it," Tony cried. "Do you dig it, Zoltan?"

"No, but she's tired and upset. For now, Tony, let's do exactly as she asks. The poor child is . . . the best thing is just for her to get to bed. So just don't say anything, if it's what Kip wants."

"All right, but I don't dig," Tony muttered.

"For tonight, just let it lie," I said. "If you don't mind, Tony. If you don't mind."

Chapter 15

"Well," Janet said, "you can rest now, and that's it. No more tedious sitting . . . or rather, standing. It's done, and your job is over, Kip."

She threw her brush across the room, spattering paint all over, and grinned.

"It's finished. I know when to stop. One more brush stroke and it will be ruined. Come and see."

We stood together, looking at the portrait of me in the Fortuny gown.

"Do you like it?" Janet asked, almost shyly.

"It's exquisite."

"Well, anyway it's a highly professional job," she said, rather self-consciously. "I don't know about exquisite."

But it was. It was a good, very good portrait and we both, being trained artists, knew it. Portraiture, after the beginning of the twentieth century, had become almost a lost art, which I had always thought a great tragedy; I had no talent for it myself, but some of the great works of art, through the centuries, had been in this genre.

I said again, "It's wonderful, superlative, Jan," and she kissed me ebulliently and said now let's celebrate.

"Tell Gertrude to give you the best bottle of scotch in the house," she cried. "We deserve it. You do and so do I. I think we have some Chivas Regal. If not that, anything else that's expensive. We'll drink it up and the devil take the hindmost."

I went downstairs and Alex was there, in the hall, looking out the window. He heard me and, as I reached the bottom, turned.

We were only inches apart.

And then, as if in a dream, he held out his arms . . . and I walked into them. There was no thought, or will. He asked for me and I went to him. His arms held me, tight against him. Our mouths didn't come together; there was no meeting of lips. He simply embraced me; I felt the texture of his jacket, smelled his light, clean, masculine smell. I felt the beating of his heart, felt his breath, warm on my face.

And then he let me go.

"It's the dress," he said. "I thought you were Janet."

"Of course," I said.

And perhaps he had. Perhaps that Fortuny dress had a special meaning for him.

Perhaps.

We nodded politely to each other. And then I continued on my way to the kitchen and got the booze from Gertrude.

When I went back to the hall there was no one there.

But I stood in the spot where Alex had held me in his arms . . . for a second or two . . . remembering.

It was only the dress, I told myself. Janet's Fortuny gown. Alex had held his young wife in his arms. It had been only that.

Did you want it to be something else? I asked myself, and had no answer.

But I stood for a moment longer.

If he had kissed me, what would it have been like?

Sooner or later, as I had known I would, I found myself alone with Alex again. I was walking along the beach and he appeared, sunglasses swinging from a hand, over the rim of a rise. He saw me at once, hesitated and then, determinedly, came down to join me.

He fell into step and I accommodated my own pace to his. "I'm stealing some time," he confided. "I left Fleur practicing Busoni. I doubt if she even knows I'm gone."

I was determined not to feel ill at ease with him. "I envy your life," I said. "It's not just you, it's those kids. You must feel very proud of what you're doing."

"You mean giving them my time? But that's the way it *has* to be. *I* was helped, and now I'm helping others. This is the way the arts are fostered."

"Who helped you?" I asked.

"A very superlative musician . . . and person," he said, and named an illustrious name. "I was never in need of financial support," he admitted. "Both Fleur and Tony are without financial backing, but that's the least of it. It's the confidence, the *cachet* an established musician gives a beginning talent. An underwriting, if

203

you will. I come from a rather stuffy New England family. None of them quite understood my aspirations. But Aaron did, and it was because of him that—"

He broke off. "But *I'm* not interesting," he said. "Fleur is. And Tony. They're the future."

"Yes, I suppose I know what you mean."

I felt hot, embarrassed and frustrated. Our conversation was so *stilted*. Art and talent and young geniuses. It was a *manufactured* conversation. I wished now that he had never joined me on the beach; I was regretful that we had been forced into this uneasy proximity. But I didn't know how to put an end to it. We kept walking along, talking in that measured, polite way, trying to hide from each other the fact that Xanadu, high on the cliff, was not the most serene of households and trying to blank out that one, brief moment when we had been physically close . . . so close that I had felt the beating of his heart.

And then suddenly everything was different. A voice hailed us from a distance and, turning, we saw the two little boys running toward us, Alex Junior and Roger. They looked like sandpipers flitting across the sand, like little, glad-hearted birds, almost as if at any moment they would flap wings and soar skywards. I turned back and saw Alex, his face joyous and delighted, one arm lifted in a buoyant salute.

"Look at those ridiculous little good-for-nothings," he said, and his voice was so changed, so changed. He was like any young husband who was proud of his offspring, just a father, just a man who was grateful for what he had been granted, two kids who meant continuity, permanence and immortality.

So he could look like this, I thought, with a pain

knifing through my heart. He could look young and happy and carefree . . .

The children caught up to us, hurled themselves at their father, and then all four of us ploughed on together across the pebbled sands. The day had suddenly lightened, as if a dark cloud had been lifted from the sky. There was no more formal talk, no carefully constructed conversation between two self-conscious adults. We played the children's games, looking for starfish, finding opalescent shells and sea stones that looked like precious jewels. And when we turned back to retrace our steps—because Alex was not on holiday even if I was—we walked four abreast, holding hands, laughing at everything and nothing as we let the salt spray drench us when the waves rolled in and broke.

I was a naturally cheerful personality, finding life from my vantage point challenging and exciting. But in this all too short hour the word "happy" assumed new proportions. With the children, with the tall, suddenly ebullient man between young Roger and me, I *knew* I was happy. I wasn't simply elated, or invigorated. I was happy and I knew it.

All this, I thought, belonged to Janet. The man, the children, the littoral life. It was hers; she held it in the palm of her hand.

But she wasn't happy.

And when we climbed the rocky scars to that house on the cliffs, the day began to darken again, though the sky remained unchanged. I looked wistfully back from where we had just come. Yonder lay the brightness and the incandescence, the innocence. And up above, on that steep and rocky cliff, was uncertainty, doubt and perverse mystery.

205

Gertrude made me a sandwich lunch. I ate it on the sundeck, listening to the sounds of music from inside and dreaming. Alex was playing piano and Fleur the violin, and it was Schubert, a composer close to my heart. The beautiful melody vibrated in the limpid air . . . and then I heard someone singing.

I hadn't heard Janet's singing voice in *so* many years.

Her voice drifted down from upstairs, and she sang in German. Jan's second language had been German; her accent had been impeccable. She had loved the tongue of Goethe and Heinrich Heine and Thomas Mann.

"It's a noble language," she used to say.

Her mezzo, rich and soaring, filled the afternoon. I listened, enchanted.

Am Brunnen vor dem Tore
Da steht ein Lindenbaum—

My cigarette smoldered, unheeded, in an ashtray. And when the song ended there were tears in my eyes. If there was such beauty in the world why, then, should there also be sadness and ugliness and horror?

It was an old, forever unresolved query. There would be both, forever, beauty and ugliness. And perhaps without the one, the other would lose impact.

I started; someone had come up the wooden steps and, with a resigned sigh, I saw that it was Dennis Sellaby. At the moment, he was the last person I wanted beside me. He gave me a quick glance, saw my half-filled plate and said he was damned hungry.

"How about feeding me?" he asked.

"Speak to Gertrude," I said shortly.

He lifted a hand. "Be right back."

In a few minutes he returned with a tray. "Shoot," he said contentedly. "Don't this look good. And scallions too."

He spread out the contents on a small table and fell to. For a while there was only the sound of his gobbling and swallowing. Then he was finished with his snack and sucking greedily at his iced coffee. "Boy, was I hungry," he said. "Where the hell's everyone?"

"Doing their thing," I said. "You and I are the only non-working slobs around the place."

"That's only temporary," he said. "Beginning after Labor Day I'll be working my butt off at Stanford U."

"Don't tell me you were accepted?" I asked.

"You think I'm retarded, don't you?"

"No, just lazy."

"Go to hell. What's that creepy music?"

It was Bach now.

"Try to like it," I said. "It's immortal."

"It sounds like practicing, a little kid practicing."

"Oh, Dennis," I said, exasperated. "It's Johann Sebastian Bach. Don't be ridiculous."

"I still think it's dishwater," he said, unabashed. "Where's Tony?"

"Writing the great American opera, I expect."

"Zoltan?"

"Working too."

"Hah! What a laugh he is. All talk and no action. He scribbles, that's all. He's taking them for a ride."

I turned on him, infuriated. "Dennis, stop talking like that. Why do you have to put on such an *act?* Don't you know that poor Zoltan is trying to justify

207

the Saxons' interest in him? Can't you be a little kind?"

"Oh, boy," he said, giving me a scornful look.

"You make me sick. Really, I mean it. That poor man. You'll get old yourself some day."

"That man?" He laughed. "Don't kid youself, sweetie. Poor? He has money in the bank. Plenty, too."

"What do you mean?" I was scornful.

"You don't believe me? All right, I'll tell you. I saw his bankbook."

"What do you mean you saw his bankbook?" I shifted impatiently.

"I did. And some other things, too. Some old papers, from abroad. From Europe. He's not Zoltan Varga at all. He took that name off of someone else. Zoltan Varga would be seventy-one years old. This guy's no chicken, but he ain't seventy-one."

"What are you *talking* about?" Oh why, I thought, couldn't I be patient with Dennis? He was only a kid, after all.

"Never mind," he said loftily. "I won't tell you."

"Then don't."

We sat for a while, and after a bit what he had said started to arouse my curiosity. What did he mean, he wasn't Zoltan Varga at all?

Zoltan Varga would be seventy-one years old . . .

"All right, what's this all about?" I asked at last.

"Go to hell."

But he saw that he had at last pricked my curiosity. His face was pleased and sly.

"Come on, Dennis, let's have it. What is it you meant?"

"Well . . ."

He began to relent. He was making me sit up and take notice, and he was clearly elated about it. He swung his feet up onto the railing and said, "I was horsing around one day, all alone in the house. I decided to see what I could find out. I read a couple of Mr. Saxon's letters, but they were nothing. Long-hair music, like that." He grinned suddenly. "I went through Mrs. Saxon's bedroom drawers. Nice undies. Lace, silk . . . very cool, keen. I dig stuff like that."

"Will you stop that disgusting drooling and come to the point!"

"So then I went nosing around Zoltan's room. And I found these old papers. You know, years and years ago. So. There was a lot of stuff, snapshots and papers, and all like that. In a foreign language. A heap of old junk."

"Well, why not? He's a European. Those are his treasures. From another life, long ago."

It fascinated me, of course. Another life, when Zoltan had been young, had been in other climes, had been . . . another man, really.

"Anyway, there was this thing, like a passport. Not like our passports, just a cardboard thing, double-folded. With Zoltan's picture. But not Zoltan."

"What do you mean not Zoltan?"

"The age, the vital statistics, as they say. Like I said, it was about an older man."

"How do you know all this? I thought it was in a foreign language?"

"It was, yeah. But the dates were there. Dates aren't in a foreign language. Whoever this guy was, that had Zoltan's picture on the passport, would be seventy-one. So you see? It was a forgery."

I realized that he was talking about a *carte d'identite*. And after a while I began to see that there *could* be a reason for a false identity card—the Iron Curtain countries, Hungary, where Zoltan came from, and the inner rebellions, the underground movements. Supposing, I thought, supposing that Zoltan, for reasons best know to himself, had wanted to become another personality. And so he paid lots of money to have a *carte d'identite* forged.

Supposing Zoltan Varga wasn't Zoltan Varga at all. Supposing he had been active in political movements, as Alex had hinted, and then after the tragic, abortive rebellion, unable to bear his own identity . . .

Who knew what ghastly things had happened. To him. To his family.

So he simply stayed Zoltan Varga, kept the identity of a dead man.

"What?" I asked, coming back to earth when Dennis said, "You're not listening."

"I said, now you know he's a load of bananas. Right?"

"A load of bananas? You mean crazy? Don't you know that millions of people, *millions*, aren't as fortunate as we are?"

"But they're *keeping* him," he said, flaring up. "And why? He's not poor. I saw the bankbook. A thousand dollars, at regular dates."

"So what about it?"

But I sat up quickly.

A thousand dollars?

"What do you mean?"

"Yeah." He flashed a triumphant smile at me. "A

thousand dollars . . . and then another thousand dollars. And another thousand dollars. Want to know what the balance is?"

The sun was terribly bright suddenly. I put a hand over my eyes. "What is the balance?" I asked, and my voice sounded like someone else's.

"Fifteen thousand," Dennis said. "Fifteen thousand and a few cents." He chuckled. "That's a lot of bread."

"You mean there were intermittent deposits of a thousand dollars?" I asked.

"Yeah, cross my heart."

A thousand dollars. The check, a cashier's check, for a thousand dollars . . .

My brain was working overtime. If Zoltan Varga hadn't always been Zoltan Varga, then it was at least likely that he could have held on to his other identity . . . for certain purposes. Like a bank account.

But that was a wrong, wrong guess. Dennis had *seen* his bankbook.

"How do you know it was Zoltan's bankbook?" I asked.

"It was in his drawer, wasn't it? Whose else could it be?"

I drew a deep breath. "Didn't you see the name on the book?"

"I saw the balance, didn't I? And it was with his other things." He looked defensive, as if in his role of private eye he had slipped up a bit.

"Then you didn't see the name on it?"

"No . . . but what does that *matter?*"

"All right, all right," I said.

"Anyway, so you see poor Zoltan's not poor at all,"

211

Dennis said, tossing the plastic straw from his coke into the bushes. "Dry your tears, baby. He's better off than you are, at least it looks that way to me."

"I don't want to talk any more about it," I said. "And if you dare say anything about this to anyone else you'll be sorry for the day you were born. You're a disgusting snoop."

I got up and went inside the house, banging the screen door.

Chapter 16

In my room I sat at the window and stared out.

I must think, I told myself. I had to think.

But my brain was in such a whirl that for a while everything milled about in my head like scattered leaves in a windstorm. Because how could anyone make *sense* of these things.

A thousand dollars.

Eugene Berne . . . Zoltan Varga.

Janet simply gave Zoltan the money, that was it! On her own, without Alex's knowing. Because she was fond of Zoltan.

But then why not pay it to Zoltan Varga? Why the subterfuge?

I started over again.

If she was paying hush money, why? What in God's name did Zoltan *have* on Janet?

He knew about Howard Dolphs?

Maybe he knew.

Even so, what woman would pay that kind of

money to keep a love affair secret? She'd simply break the affair off, admit the truth to her husband and start being a good girl again. Any decent man would be able to come to terms with an indiscretion on his wife's part . . . and Alex was certainly a decent man.

I got up and walked around and lit a cigarette and looked at myself in the mirror and then sat down again, resolutely, getting a grip on myself.

Because I had to unscramble this. I *had* to.

There was a whirling sound in the sky and the chopper went by again, overhead, with its proselytizing banner streaming against the sky.

ADOPT A CHILD.

I watched it until it was out of sight and I don't know why, but it seemed to be saying something to me. Something that was fluttering inside my mind. Trying to get through to me, to reach the surface, to . . .

To get through.

ADOPT A CHILD.

And then I got up abruptly and went over to a small writing desk and pulled some notepaper out of the drawer. Notepaper that had XANADU printed at the top. I started writing aimlessly, just putting down anything that came into my head. I wrote: Adopt a child, a thousand dollars, Eugene Berne, Zoltan Varga, adopt a child.

And then my pen stopped and my thoughts began, turgidly at first, to organize themselves.

You see, I was thinking, it must have all started way back, when Jan and Alex were first married. Maybe a month, maybe two months, three or four . . .

But it must have started then. When Alex had turned to Miriam Sellaby. His wife had declined to go with him to Europe for that musical tour . . . and when he had come back she hadn't been there, but was somewhere else. Even her parents didn't know where.

"I knew it was touch and go then," Alex had said.

All right, take it from there. Janet had met that woman in Morro Bay, Mrs. Morris. Who had told me, *"Janet and I shared a common tragedy . . ."*

I was a woman, after all. And one of the worst tragedies that could befall a woman was to lose her child. Either through miscarriage, death, or abortion.

Or if she didn't have an abortion.

But instead had the baby and gave it away.

And somebody else had adopted it.

It was like a crossword puzzle. You knew the words, only they eluded you; you blanked out when it came to the crucial point. A six letter word for—

Of course you knew the word. Only you blanked out.

ADOPT A CHILD.

And then, as it happened with crossword puzzles, something came dimly to me. Fleur and Tony. They hadn't been adopted by Alex, but they were here, under his aegis . . . they were almost like adopted children.

Fleur!

I felt my heart flutter in my chest.

Fleur.

"Hers is rather a sad story," Alex had told me. "She's an orphan . . ."

And then I started writing frantically. With dates, figuring the here and now . . . 1971 . . . and what had gone before. Janet and Alex had been married for . . . let's say, fourteen years. And Fleur was thirteen.

I scribbled figures, subtracted, and came up with a possible answer. If Fleur had been born while Alex was away in Europe on that concert tour, then she would be, now, about the age I'd been told she was.

Thirteen.

My next thought, as my heart pounded was, *that man in San Francisco.*

After a while I put aside paper and pen and sat thinking soberly, unbelieving. Suppose Janet had been pregnant when she married Alex. So? Why not simply tell him? Throw herself on his mercy?

An intelligent woman . . . an intelligent man.

What idiot of a woman would let herself be the blackmailed victim of someone just because of a tragic mistake in her past?

And who *was* Zoltan, that he had found out about it?

Fleur . . . why should I think of Fleur?

It was the hair . . . that bright head . . . like Howard's!

But it was impossible! How could it be?

I went through the motions of the rest of the day.

Until that evening, when they were all out on the sundeck at cocktail time. I made some excuse and slipped away. Heart in mouth, I went into Zoltan's room.

I was almost suffocated with trepidation as I started quietly opening drawers. I hadn't dared close the door behind me; otherwise I couldn't have heard the approach of anyone who might have taken it into his or her head to come upstairs. I rummaged, taking care to slip out only a few things at a time.

I began to sweat. This kind of thing was not my style. And after a while, as the minutes slipped by, I felt like crying. It was like looking for a needle in a haystack. There were handkerchiefs, socks, shirts, underthings . . . it was obscene, what I was doing.

And then my fraying patience was rewarded. I came across a leather-bound writing tablet. It was a combination pad, pencil and address book; its cover, maroon with gilt stenciling and very worn and old, was initialed.

The initials were E.B.

For a moment I felt faint, and I gripped the top of the chest. E.B.

Eugene Berne.

The letters burned themselves into my mind.

E.B.

My God, it can't be, I thought dizzily. *It can't be.*

But there it was. It was right there, under my nose, in Zoltan's chest. The evidence. And then, feverishly, I searched for the bankbook. And found it. In a small blue envelope. I slid the book out of the pasteboard envelope and looked at it.

It was all the proof I needed. The name on the bankbook was Eugene Berne.

I riffled quickly through it.

The first deposit was made in March of 1966.

A few months later another deposit was listed and, after that, at irregular intervals, other deposits.

The last one had been made only a few days ago.

I flipped the pages over and glanced at the balance.

Dennis had told the truth. The balance was $15,026.

I put everything quickly in order again, frantic with haste and fear. My legs were like rubber and my hands were shaking so that when I closed the drawer I knocked an ancient-looking, silver-handled brush off the top of the chest. And gasped, stifling a scream.

I picked it up and put it back and knocked it off a second time.

When I left the room I felt as if I was going to have a heart attack.

I could scarcely breathe.

I dashed down the hall to my room and bathed my feverish face, held my arms under the water. Other things were falling into place. Now my thoughts couldn't come quickly enough.

When Zoltan and I had driven into San Francisco.

My God, it could have been Zoltan who'd attacked me on the street! In the crowd he would have been able to—

And the doll . . .

Zoltan!

Of course, of course . . . that first morning, when I had telephoned to Norma . . . the click . . . someone *had* been listening in. Zoltan.

And then he got frightened. The things I'd said to Norma . . . *"I won't leave here until I get to the bottom of whatever it is."*

He thought he could scare me away. First by dismembering my doll and then by giving me a fright in the street in Chinatown.

That was, if he hadn't meant to really kill me, as he had killed Olympia.

218

And as he was slowly but surely killing Janet.

How long before her mind would snap?

And then I started to laugh. It was hysteria, of course. It was the sheer insanity of it, all of it. There weren't people like that! People who were learned and quietly philosophical and brilliantly rational . . . men like *that* couldn't do things like blackmail a decent woman, a *benefactress,* for God's sake. Only a twisted mind could take such devious means . . . and wielding a *knife? Zoltan??*

Not Zoltan. Not Zoltan Varga, I reminded myself. Someone else who used that name. Someone who, because of possibly terrible things in his past life, *did* have a twisted mind. A paranoid, no matter how gentle and gossipy and benign he seemed on the surface. Someone with a bone to pick . . . against life.

When I went down again Fleur was just starting up the flight. "Oh, Kip," she said, "are you all right?"

"Yes, certainly. Why?"

"Well, you were gone so long."

"Was I?" I smiled a rather strained smile. "I think I got too much sun today. I came up to take a couple of aspirins."

"Feeling better now?"

"I will in a little while. Nothing to worry about, Fleur."

"Dinner's ready," she said, and I followed her outdoors.

We were in the middle of the meal when I thought of something else.

The man from San Francisco taking pictures on the beach. Jan's two little boys . . . and someone else.

219

Fleur.

"Kip?"

Tony waved a hand in front of my face.

I came back to earth.

"Where were you, what planet?" he asked.

"Uh . . ."

"Want some more wine?"

"Oh yes, thanks."

I sipped it, but I didn't taste it at all. I couldn't have said what we'd had for dinner. Or what we'd talked about.

Not the children, not Alex Junior or Roger, I thought. He hadn't been taking pictures of Jan's children.

He'd been taking pictures of Fleur.

Chapter 17

I waited until the next day. And then, after hesitating for hours, went up to Jan's studio. She was setting a charcoal sketch, spraying on the fixative. "May I come in?" I asked.

"Sure. How's everything around the place today?"

"Could we talk?"

"Talk? Why not? Let's have a cigarette."

We lit up and I said, "Janet, I've skirted around this until now. But today, this afternoon, I want to get down to cases. I want to know what's bugging you."

She blinked and then attempted a laugh. "My word, we *do* sound serious," she said.

"Stop it," I cried. "Janet, will you please take off that other face you've been wearing and *talk to me!*"

For some time her face was downcast. Her long hair swept across her cheeks; her eyes were hidden from me. "No, it's no use," she said after a while. "Don't say any more, Kip."

"Yes, I will. Oh yes, I will. Tell me, Janet. I want

to help you. And I've been so sure that you wanted my help. I'm not going to drop the subject. I *have* to help. It's important to me. After all, that's why I came here, to see what the trouble was."

Her head shot up. "What do you mean by that?" she demanded, her eyes shocked. "You came here to—"

I fell silent.

"What's been going on behind my back?" she asked harshly, and stood up. "You came here to help? Who asked you?"

"Janet, please." I stood up too, and we faced each other. "I tell you I know about it! I know someone's taking money from you. A thousand dollars, regularly."

She gasped, and her face was the color of paper.

"What?" she said, thinly.

"Yes, I know about it."

"How, *how?*" Her eyes stared at me, dark and incredulous. *"How* do you know these things? These dark, dirty, sordid facts of my life. *How do you know?"*

I was trembling. "I've been so worried," I said. "I had to find out. Don't you see? It's what I came for. Because I was told that—"

"You were told . . . who told you?" she asked whitely.

"That doesn't matter. Janet, level with me. Tell me!"

"No no," she said, brushing my outstretched hand away. "From whom did you learn this?"

"I saw his bankbook."

"Whose bankbook?"

"Zoltan's!"

I put my hands on her shoulders as she sagged. "You *didn't* know it was him, did you? But it is. That fascinating, brilliant man. You didn't know who the culprit was, of course not. But it was Zoltan! He's such a brilliant man that he could do a thing like this to you, his benefactress, his—"

She looked at me and her face was ashen. There was a beading of moisture on her forehead and upper lip. "Zoltan," she whispered. "Why, you're crazy. You're . . ."

"No, I'm not. So you didn't guess. But now I'm telling you. It's Zoltan. I was in his room, I saw his belongings. And the bankbook. The cashier's check you'd written out for a thousand dollars. You've been paying money to someone you thought was a friend."

She said, as if hypnotized, "Zoltan, Zoltan? *Zoltan?*"

Her face went a kind of ghastly yellow.

"Yes. Now will you talk it over with me? Now, will you—"

"Zoltan," she whispered. "Oh, please God, no."

I saw her eyes move past me. There was a sudden look of shocked concern on her face. I turned and saw what she saw. Small Roger was standing in the doorway, his expression grave and troubled. His lower lip was trembling.

"Roger," Janet said. "Darling, how long have you been standing there?"

"Are you and Kip having a fight?"

"No no . . ." She went to him, knelt, put her arms around him. At once he started to cry. "Oh no, don't, don't," Janet crooned. "Darling baby, Mommy's not having a fight with Kip. We were having a *discussion*.

We're old friends, you see, and . . . well, there was something we had to talk out."

The child continued to cry. Janet held him in her arms and rocked him. "Oh, baby," she said softly. "Dear baby. I'm a bad Mommy. I'm a terrible Mommy. Such a bad Mommy . . ."

"What's all this commotion?" Alex asked, running up the steps. "Did Rog hurt himself?"

"It's all right," Janet said. "Just a misunderstanding. Alex, see to the children, will you? Tell Gertrude to take over for the rest of the day."

She smiled at the little boy and said, "Gertrude will let you have ice cream sticks. That's nice, isn't it? And you won't be mad at me? Mommy wants to go to bed."

"For a nap?"

"Yes, because I have a headache."

"Is it a bad one?" he asked seriously.

"A very bad one."

Over his head, as she clasped him to her again, I saw the tears diffuse Janet's eyes. Her lovely face was agonized. "Okay, run along now," she said. "Tell Gertrude about the popsicles."

"Groovy," Roger said. He ran off, his tears drying.

"Have you really got a headache?" Alex asked.

"Have I got a headache. I could die with this headache. If all the bad heads in the world were lined up in a row, mine would stand up and sneer at the rest of them." She laughed shrilly. "That's an old line from a Thirties picture. William Gargan was the butler. I've seen it a hundred times on TV." She looked at her husband in a kind of dazed way. "Yes, I have a headache," she said quietly. "And I don't want to be dis-

224

turbed for hours and hours, is that clearly understood?"

He said just as quietly, "Isn't there something I can do?"

"Nothing. Nothing anyone can do. Nothing at all."

She went off and I listened to her going downstairs. "What happened?" Alex asked me.

He saw how shaken I was and waited. I had this terrible feeling that I had made things a hundred times worse. That I had laid the last burden across Janet's back. By trying to help I had made things worse . . . very much worse. Every nerve was screaming. What had I done . . . the do-gooder . . . *what had I done?*

He finally got me calmed down. He was patient, waiting, smoking quietly, and then I told him about Zoltan, about what I'd learned from Dennis. "Apparently Zoltan knows something about Jan," I said. "Something she wants to . . . to keep secret."

He shook his head, as if he were trying to clear it of a fog so that he could begin to absorb what I'd said. "*Dennis* told you this?"

"He'd been snooping. He's evidently that kind of person. He was in Zoltan's room and found a bankbook. There have been fairly regular deposits in the amount of a thousand dollars each . . . and the balance is a little over fifteen thousand."

"You can't mean this," Alex said.

"Obviously Janet had no idea to whom she was paying the money. It was just a name, a name she had no way of tracing. You must believe it, Alex. If you want to help your wife."

There was a long silence and then he said, "Go on."

225

"Zoltan also seems to have two identities. Dennis found that out as well." I repeated the story the boy had told me. "And then, Alex, everything began to fall into place. Because I myself saw a cashier's check Janet had drawn, for a thousand dollars, and I saw the envelope alongside it. There was a San Francisco box number and a name I later looked up in the San Francisco phone book. There was no one by that name listed."

I had a sudden wild hope. "Do you know a Eugene Berne?" I asked.

He shook his head. "No. I've never heard the name."

The feeble hope died down. I went doggedly on. "After Dennis told me about the bankbook I did some snooping of my own. It was a horrible thing to do, but I had to do it. In one of Zoltan's drawers was a leather address book, an old and much-used one. With the initials E.B. And I saw the bankbook. What Dennis said was correct."

My voice choked up with the last words and I turned away.

When I looked back he was gripping the cane back of a chair, his knuckles white. And I had to be the one to tell him this, I thought bitterly.

"Zoltan's dangerous," I said tiredly. "There were certain things he found out . . . about my concern for Janet. I have, unfortunately, a big mouth. It was just that . . . I thought there was one person I could trust . . . an older man, a wise man." I laughed shortly. "Anyway, that's what I thought."

"Obviously he's dangerous," Alex said. There was

no expression on his face; it was blank. Only his eyes . . .

"He's doubly dangerous," I said. "He's not only a thief, the worst kind of thief, but he's tried to give me a couple of good scares. Because he must have realized I was getting too close to the truth."

"What do you mean, tried to give you—"

I told him about the doll. And about the incident in Chinatown. "He's terrified of being found out. Think what it would mean for him. Worse than anything, the disgrace. The final blow from life. He's despicable and I want to light matches under his fingernails. But that proud, vain man . . . it will kill him."

"Better so," Alex said, and I saw the first sign of rage and hate on his face. And his color had bettered. The ghastly pallor lessened and he was beginning to gain control of himself. He was beginning to believe my terrible story. He was beginning to absorb it. He was beginning to get used to it.

It was incredible how you refused to accept something frightful and then, almost instantly credited it and, finally, gathered together your forces to deal with it. It was a hidden reserve inside almost all of us, something you didn't even realize was there, until you had need of it.

"What will you do?" I asked.

"Do? Why, I must talk to Janet, of course." He passed a hand across his hair, tiredly. "Poor girl," he said after a while. "I don't understand why. I don't understand. I wouldn't ever hurt Janet. How is it she doesn't know that?"

Because, I thought, it seemed that there was some-

227

one Janet felt that same way about, the way Alex felt about Janet. Someone she loved, truly loved, had never stopped loving.

She had been faithful to Alex, like Cynara, only in her fashion.

"Well," he finally said, in a new, brisk way that indicated he was planning his strategy. "As for this evening, we must do something about that. One step at a time. I won't be downstairs with the rest, and will simply say Janet isn't well, that I'll have a tray with her. As for you, Katherine, you won't want to sit down to table with Zoltan, I'm sure."

"I'd rather not. It was very difficult last night, knowing what I did."

"Then why don't you take one of the cars and drive to Monterey? You can spend the afternoon there and have dinner on the wharf. I'll tell the others you were to meet a friend there, some visitor from New York."

It was a relief to be talking about mundane things this way, to swing into action. It was a relief to have the wonder and the uncertainty cleared up. I would go to Monterey and it was Alex's guess that Janet should pull out of her psychogenic migraine in about six hours. "She has special medication that puts her right to sleep," he told me. "And then, when she wakes up . . ."

He took a deep breath.

"You run along now, Katherine. I'm going to take myself a long, long walk. I have a lot of thinking to do. And thank you, thank you. For telling me all this. It must have been very difficult for you."

I choked up again, nodded blindly, and left him.

Chapter 18

I pulled out of the driveway quietly, in the Triumph, and was in Monterey inside of half an hour. I decided I needed a stiff drink, and had a scotch and soda, plus several nervous cigarettes, at a place on the wharf. Afterwards, I did some shopping in some of the touristy gift shops, bought something very pretty for Norma, had it sent to her address, and treated myself to a frozen custard. There wasn't much to do but wander and window shop, and out of ennui I bought something for myself, a sterling silver brooch I thought would go well with one or two of my fall suits.

After that I looked at my watch again. It was only three o'clock.

The Monterey wharf, a smaller edition of Fisherman's Wharf in San Francisco, was exhausted very quickly. Or so I thought until I came across a curious little shop where they traded in occult books. The exterior tempted me mildly, but when I went in and talked with the proprietors, my interest was more keenly aroused.

I thought that the people who ran the place might very well be witches. And there were fascinating things there; esoterica, strange, arcane literature that would, I thought, cause the prominent nose of Dr. Farthing, my Lit professor at the University, to flare at the nostrils. Professor Farthing had introduced me to a number of obscure French, German and Russian writers whose tales of deviltry were wonderfully macabre. He was a specialist in the cabalistic and the recondite. And after rummaging around, attended by one of the spooky proprietors, I found a book called *MERVIN MERVIN*, by an eighteenth century German author with the appropriate name of Rudolf Grabscheid (the last name means "grave-digger") and had it mailed to Dr. Farthing with my card.

When I went out into the sunlight again, after the gloom of the dusty-windowed book store, I looked at my watch and it was only a quarter to five.

Too early for dinner. And anyway, I had no appetite at all. The thought of food gagged me. And it would be hours and hours before the meal ended at Xanadu. There would be drinks, with dinner not sooner than seven or later.

I had so much *time* to kill.

And then I stood still, thinking. Because it had suddenly come to me that I didn't want to go back at all. I didn't want to return to Xanadu. It seemed to me that, now everything had begun coming out into the open, I was no longer in the picture. I didn't belong now. It was Alex's business, not really mine. No matter how much I loved Janet and remembered our common, youthful past, she was married to Alex. Her life had gone beyond mine.

I made up my mind. I would get a room somewhere . . . wherever there were motels. I didn't even have to go back ever. I could ask for my things to be sent on to Manhattan. Janet had a husband, a life. She didn't need me now. Neither of them needed me. I would only be an embarrassment.

It was five o'clock when I called the house.

There was a long wait before the phone was picked up. Then the last ring was cut off abruptly and I heard Gertrude's voice.

"May I speak to Mr. Saxon, Gertrude?" I asked. "This is Kip."

"Oh, Miss Kip . . . something terrible, Missy. Something terrible."

"*What?* What's terrible, Gertrude?"

I could hear her trying to control her tremulous voice, trying to stick to the King's English, trying to be calm. There was a snuffle of sorts. I plastered my ear to the receiver. "Gertrude? Gertrude!" I cried. "Are you there? Speak to me!"

"Missy Janet gone," she said quaveringly.

"What do you mean *gone?*" I demanded, sweating in the stuffy booth.

"Yes, gone. Her room empty, that's all." She broke into sobbing. "Something terrible going on here, Kip."

She wept, the sound of her sobs rhythmical over the phone. "Ah ah ah ah . . ."

"When?" I asked tersely, and then shouted it. *"When did she go?"*

"Maybe an hour, maybe two hour. Just gone . . ." And the ah ah ah ah came again.

231

I put a hand against the wall to steady myself. "But where would she go?"

"I don't know. Where? I don't know. Ah ah ah ah . . ."

"Gertrude, now listen to me carefully. Did she and Mr. Saxon have words? I mean, was there a fight? Or anything like that?"

"No no. Mr. Saxon go up to her room. But Mrs. Janet wasn't there. Kip? Where are you, Kip?"

"I'm in Monterey," I said. "Darling, let me talk to Alex. To Mr. Saxon."

"He's gone too," she said desolately.

"Where'd he *go?*"

"Everyone gone," she said wildly. "I don't know where Mr. Alex is!"

"Where's Zoltan?" I asked, filled with foreboding.

"Gone," she said dramatically. "I *said*, Kip, *every-one* gone!"

"What? Are the children alone there?"

"Not alone," she said. "I'm here, and Tony and Miss Fleur. And Mr. Lance and Mrs. Lance. Mr. Saxon call them and say come over because he have to go somewhere."

"Let me talk to Mrs. Lance. Please hurry, Gertrude."

But before she could come to the phone my call ran out. I slipped another coin into the slot and called again. It was Mrs. Lance who answered. "I'm in a toll booth," I said rapidly. "I'll have to make this fairly brief."

"Yes, Kip," she said calmly and, although I didn't give it a thought at the time, remembered it later. No

232

hysterics, no cuteness, no tears. "Where are you, dear?"

"I'm in Monterey. I called because I wanted to know the progress of things there. Mrs. Lance, what's going on?"

"Everything," she said in that calm voice. "The sky's fallen. Janet's disappeared and Alex has gone after her."

"Where has he gone?"

"Why, to that house on Ghiradelli Square," she said, and now her voice sounded a little tired, a little defeated. "He feels she must have headed for there and so do I."

"He knows about that? Alex knows about . . . about that?"

"He does now," Mrs. Lance said. "Under the circumstances, there was only one thing to do. Therefore I did it. I told him."

"Oh."

So Mrs. Lance had known about it too. Well, she had certainly fooled *me*. She'd known about it all the time. "Where's Zoltan?" I asked.

"What does it matter about Zoltan?" she asked, with a strange little laugh. "I don't know where he is and I must say I don't particularly care."

"But it *does* matter about him," I cried. "It matters terribly, Mrs. Lance. He's been blackmailing Janet. Didn't Alex tell you? And—"

I broke off. From the glass door of the booth I saw, suddenly, a man walking along the wharf, a man I recognized instantly. It was Zoltan, and he was looking from left to right, clearly searching for something . . . or someone.

233

Me, I thought, feeling cold. He was looking for me.

"Mrs. Lance," I said hurriedly, "don't worry about Zoltan. He's here, in Monterey. Someone must have told him I'd come here. I must get away. But guard the children. Please keep them safe. I don't know what—" I became incomprehensible. "I don't know what he'd do. He's already tried to —"

"Your three minutes are up," an operator intoned. "Please deposit another coin in the slot."

"Kip . . . wait . . . Kip . . ." Mrs. Lance sounded frantic.

"There's not time," I said. "I have to get away. He mustn't see me. I suppose he's determined to find me." I heard my own wild laughter. "I don't relish being knifed to death in this phone booth."

"Kip!"

"I have to hang up. Take care of the children. I love you," I said insanely, and hung up the phone. I cringed against the side of the smelly, stifling booth, but Zoltan passed right by without seeing me. He was plodding along, in that duck walk of his, looking, surveying, his eyes sharp and penetrating . . . but he didn't spot me in the phone booth.

I waited until he was well past the booth, then slid out, dashed in the opposite direction, found my car, unlocked it and climbed in. "My God," I was mumbling as I put the car in gear and slid away from my parking space. "That it should come to this."

I wasn't even sure what I meant by it. I only knew that I was in the middle of a melodrama, that anything could happen now and that if Zoltan saw me driving away he'd race back to his own car and follow me.

"Don't," I prayed to God, or gods, or good fairies. "Don't let him see me."

I forked out onto the road, pressed my foot down on the gas pedal and let her go. I knew my destination. She must be there, I told myself. Janet hadn't taken any medication, had only faked a headache. She *must* have gone to Ghiradelli Square, her last refuge.

I had a straight road until I came to Santa Cruz, where I had to cut off for the Expressway. From then on I ran into difficulties. It was rush hour now; people were returning home from the day's work. It was a lousy time to be on the road; there was an enormous amount of traffic coming and going.

The steady stream of cars dazed me. I wasn't used to driving in traffic like this. I had never owned a car in New York. Every small delay set my teeth on edge. And what I hadn't counted on was darkness. But it seemed to me that if I kept crawling along at this snail's pace, it would be night before I got where I was heading. And then the worst thing of all that could happen happened: there was an accident on the road. It created a bottle-neck; there was a cop diverting traffic into another lane . . . and then as I waited, tapping impatiently with my foot hovering over the gas pedal, I saw a red Mustang in my rear view mirror. It was a few cars behind me, on the farther lane, and I couldn't see the driver . . . but I *could* see, with a shock of horror, the small, flower-shaped decal on the front left fender.

There was just such a decal on the Xanadu Mustang.

I felt moisture spring to my hot face. He had followed me, then. Zoltan had seen me in Monterey, after all, and here he was, close on my heels, practically tail-gating.

My vivid imagination told me the whole story. He had drowned Janet and killed Alex, who was missing along with Janet. And now he was after me. I was to be the next victim. And I remembered how I'd admired him. How I'd respected him. His charm, his erudition . . . yet under that *gemutlich* exterior, the fun-loving, beer-drinking, music-worshiping exterior, was a man I didn't know. Someone violent and cruel. Someone dangerous.

I got past the road block and put my foot down. Elatedly, I saw that the Mustang was still held in check. Luck, I thought . . . blind, fantastic luck . . . and then, as if a mechanical device had pulled a switch somewhere, night fell. Lights blazed on the Expressway stanchions; the dusky sky lost its last color and became opaque, as much from fog as from the coming of the dark.

And now the night was a shroud. I felt blind, impotent . . . the miles crawled by. The children, I thought. Let the children be safe. And Janet. Zoltan hadn't drowned her, I knew; it was only my fevered imagination. Let Janet be safe, and Alex, of whom I was so fond.

Savagely, I amended the last cowardly statement. You hypocrite, I told myself, not fond. You love him. Love Alex, who is Janet's husband. Other women had found themselves in the same bind, the same terrible trap. I felt his arms around me, felt his warm breath on my cheek.

The lights of the city lit up the road suddenly, and

then I saw the cut-off I had to take. I swerved, on two wheels now, and as I had been doing, peered once again through the rear view mirror for a glimpse of a red Mustang. My heart plummeted . . . and then settled again. No, that was a larger car, and there were three people inside. Just the same, that flesh of red unnerved me, and now I had an entirely new train of thought. *That* car wasn't the one, but just the same Zoltan couldn't be very far behind. And in a horrible flash the scene imprinted itself on my mind. I would park the car, dash up to the house, find it in darkness . . . and the other car would pull up in back of mine. Zoltan would get out . . .

I could hear, as if it had already happened, the slam of his car door. I could hear his heavy steps coming toward me.

I would be all alone. It would be an unseen struggle in the dark.

Someone has to help me, I thought. *It couldn't happen like that* . . .

But it could. It could happen exactly like that. Alone, in the darkness, overpowered, my throat cut.

Chapter 19

It was almost nine when I pulled up in front of the house on Bay Street. I couldn't believe my good fortune. There was a light on in the front lower apartment. Thank God, I thought. Thank God.

There was one more tense moment. The light was on, yes. He could be out, though. But he was home. At my ring, a buzzer sounded, and I opened the downstairs door in the small vestibule. When I went inside I pressed the button in front of 1A and waited. Soon the door was opened.

I tumbled in and said, "Hello, I was just afraid you might not be here. I thought you might have taken Janet somewhere else."

It was so wonderful that there was light here, and that everything was all right. I wasn't afraid any more. I wasn't alone now. "You must forgive me," I said quickly. "But you understand, I suppose."

I looked up at him.

"Please forgive me," I said. "I'm in a bit of trouble. You see—"

I was looking around; I couldn't help my curiosity, because this was where Janet had spent so much of her time. It was a large living room with high ceilings which had beautiful plaster ornamentations. There was a handsome fireplace with a gilt-framed pier glass over its mantel. There was a marble-topped coffee table on which rested a cut-glass vase filled with lilacs.

The heavy scent of the blooms perfumed the room, was almost overpowering. "I'm Katherine Cornwall," I said, turning my attention to the man in whose apartment I was. The man Janet had, apparently, loved for many years. I felt a little humble. If she loved him, he must be a very unusual man.

He was certainly fine-looking. Yes, prepossessing, with that wealth of golden hair and those timeless, sculptured features. His eyes might have been the eyes of a Renaissance model in a Da Vinci painting.

I apologized again. "I'm so sorry to burst in at this hour," I said. "I'm Katherine Cornwall," I repeated. "A friend of Janet's. I'm staying at Xanadu."

"Yes, I know who you are," he said.

"Is she here?"

He looked down at me. "Here?"

"Please," I said. "You must trust me. I don't ask anything. I only want to know if she's all right. That's absolutely all."

"But what makes you think she'd be here?"

I read his expression for one of annoyance, embarrassment. "Oh, please," I said. "There's no time for dissembling. I've been followed ever since I left Monterey. You can trust me, *honestly*. You see, Mr.

Dolphs, I found out—never mind how—that Janet has been blackmailed. His name is Zoltan Varga and he's living with the Saxon's and—"

I put a hand to my head. He was so damned *unresponsive*, so—

The two of us were standing there in the middle of the room and he didn't move, or look sympathetic, or worried, or—

He just stood there, that wonderful-looking man, with his beautiful hair, his . . . his *beauty*. And then he said, "How did you learn this?"

"I . . . oh, does it matter? Isn't it enough that this terrible thing has been happening to her? And that this Zoltan . . . who isn't Zoltan at all, but somebody else . . . realizes that I *know*. And he's on my trail."

Part of me was listening for the sound of a car stopping in front of the house. "Please stop looking at me as if I were a hysterical female," I begged. "I tell you I was *attacked* here in San Francisco. On the street. Yes, in Chinatown. Long before I found out about Zoltan's activities . . ."

A small, nagging part of my brain listened to what I had just said. *Long before I found out about Zoltan's activities* . . . It leapt out at me sharply and then was lost as I rushed on. "I told Janet about Zoltan. Well, what would you have done? I had to let her know. I was telling her and our voices were loud and then her little boy was standing in the doorway. We hadn't seen him. He . . . she . . ."

I remembered vividly, oh, so vividly. Janet with her arms around Roger, rocking him. *"I'm a bad Mommy. Such a bad Mommy . . ."*

"I can't waste any more time," I said. "There's no

241

use in pretending with me. I know too much for you to—"

"How did you find out about Zoltan?" he asked.

I couldn't believe his stupidity. I was telling him about Janet's difficulties, telling him how worried I was about her . . . and about my own danger, and he was only interested in how I had learned what I had. It was like a ghastly dream, this unfamiliar room, silent, cloistered, this tall, strange-looking, handsome man, this hidden, secret life. I felt smothered, and the scent of the flowers in the crystal vase choked me.

"I want to see Janet," I cried. "Please, please."

He shook his head.

"But she's here! She's here, isn't she?"

I was suddenly afraid. Afraid that, after all, Janet wasn't behind one of those closed doors, afraid that I had made a dreadful mistake, afraid of the encircling walls, afraid of my own isolation . . .

Then something came to me. Zoltan . . . he had said the name familiarly enough.

"Do you know Zoltan?" I asked.

"Yes, of course."

"You do? How?"

"He used to live here, in 1C."

"1C?" I repeated it stupidly.

"He was our friend."

"Your friend?"

It began to sound like a broken record. It was sur-realistic, like one of those endless, unpeopled land-scapes, with a bent crutch that meant nothing . . . and everything.

I suddenly laughed. "Your friend is a poor excuse for a friend," I said. "He's a—"

"After she left, he kept me going. I would do anything for him."

"After who left?"

"Janet, of course." A contemptuous look changed his face. He didn't look so handsome now. "She's my wife."

"Your *what?*"

"She belonged to me. We lived together. We have a child, *our* child. She married him, but she couldn't forget me. She had to come back. And back. Because I'm the real part of her life."

"You were never married to her, were you?"

"What does a piece of paper mean?" He glared at me. "Is that important? She cheated me. She said when he came back from Europe that she'd tell him, get a divorce. She had my child inside her."

And then one last, blinding truth came home to me. It was so crushing, so sad and so fantastic that I felt, for the first time, pity for this man as well as the others, Janet and Alex.

"When was she carrying your child," I asked quietly. "After she had married Mr. Saxon?"

There was a long, long silence.

"After," he said, his face breaking. "After. That's the whole point. That I could never prove anything."

I stepped back. No wonder, I thought. No wonder Janet let herself be blackmailed. It would have been worth any woman to pay the money. A bride . . . impregnated by another man.

A *bride.*

"She cheated me," Howard said again. "She didn't get a divorce. She left me *again.* And then at last I heard from her. She was home again, I mean at *that*

243

place, out there. She told me the baby died. I didn't believe her but . . . sometimes I believed her . . . and . . ."

He leaned against the mantel. "Then at last, oh, not very long ago, I knew she'd been lying. The baby hadn't died. No no. She trapped herself, Janet did. Little things she said, and then Zoltan guessed the truth. It wasn't hard to find out what happened. And then I saw with my own eyes."

His gaze was far-seeing. "I know my child. A man recognizes his own child."

He turned his face away, but not before I saw the consummate grief and hopelessness in it. He held up his hands. "I tried to kill myself," he said dispassionately. "Zoltan found me before I was out of it. I won't forgive him for that part of it. There are plenty of things I'll never forgive, one of them being on the short end of the receiving line when it comes to luck. It's in the genes, I suppose. You look around you. All the millions of people. Some of them lucky, some unlucky . . . always unlucky."

"I'm so sorry," I said. "I'm really so sorry. Fleur's your child, isn't she?"

He nodded.

"Did Janet finally say she was?"

"No, but she didn't have to. She said it with her eyes."

"I want to talk to her. Just for a minute. Just to tell her I understand now, and that I'm sorry."

I was totally unprepared for his reaction to this. To what I'd just said. It was so unexpected.

His eyes blazed at me. "Sorry? After what you've done?"

244

"What *I've* done?"

"What you've done! It would never have happened. Everything would have come out all right. Zoltan would have piled up enough to last him for the few years he has left. But trust my rotten luck! *You* had to come here and—"

"Dear God, what in the world did *I* have to do with it?" I crashed my hand down on the back of a chair, felt the pain splinter up into my elbow. And yet, way down deep in my mind, I knew I was protesting too much. That yes, I *had* been the one to bring everything to light. Yes, there was a certain kind of guilt and yes, I had played God. Out of good intentions, but just the same . . .

However, I rushed on. "An evil way of life," I said savagely. "What kind of animal are you? And Zoltan? Driving a poor, unhappy woman to distraction . . ."

I said loudly, "Where is she? You must know where she is. If you didn't, you'd be frantic, the way I am. You profess to love her!"

He came toward me. "What's happened is your fault. I knew right away, when Janet told me who you were, what you meant to her, that there would be trouble. 'Once I was innocent and untouched,' she told me. 'There was a time when everything was perfect and beautiful.' She tried to go back. But you can never go back. If you hadn't come here, everything would have worked out for me . . . for us . . ."

He bore down on me, his face dark and tormented. "It's speople like you who are dangerous," he said. "You came here and ruined our lives. I would have been able to fix everything. Janet's husband would have met with an accident. She would have been free.

245

Everything would have worked out just the way I wanted it. All I needed was time, a little time."

He looked a little dazed suddenly, and I saw his eyes, for perhaps a split second, roll in his head. What he had just said echoed against the walls.

Janet's husband would have met with an accident . . .

Why, he was . . .

"You're . . . why, you're—"

"What?" he asked thinly, and took another step forward.

"Nothing. I just—"

His eyes . . .

There was a lurch in my chest.

His eyes . . .

I looked up into them, and now I knew what fear was like. Blind, desperate fear. Of course he was sick . . . crazy. He was stark, staring mad. My eyes darted around the room . . . *if I could get out that door . . .*

He anticipated my move. In one swift movement he had interposed himself between me and my exit. I heard my own accelerated breathing, and said the first thing that come into my head. "I can't stand that faucet," I breathed. "Can't you fix that leaky faucet?"

There was a brief silence. I watched his attention swerve to the dull drip drip from somewhere beyond the room. He nodded, listening, and then said, almost defensively, "These are old houses. There are other nuisances besides leaky faucets."

"But these things are simple to attend to," I said. "You need a new washer, that's all." I was only stalling for time, which had suddenly become very precious. I knew, of course, knew fully what I was up

246

against. I was alone and closeted with a psychopath. There was no longer any doubt in my mind. Like most college-educated persons I had been shown, in Abnormal Psych courses, through insane asylums. I knew what these personalities were capable of.

He shook his head irritably and I felt my face crumple. All the nightmares I had ever had merged together into this one gigantic nightmare. It was night, and I was in a strange city all alone, confined in a high-ceilinged, deathly quiet room with a man who had no conscience . . . because he was sick, mindless . . .

For one blinding, terrible moment I wondered if after all *I* was sick, dreaming . . .

Then I heard it again, that full-throated, hollow drip. I think there are perceptions deep within us which most of the time lie slumbering . . . most of the time . . . but when one is on the ragged edge, every nerve exposed . . . then this sixth, mysterious sense becomes strangely acute . . .

I was aware of my own actions, even of my facial expressions. I was *conscious* of my eyes widening, my pupils dilating. I felt the thick barrier that stood, for a shocked, sickening moment, between me and impetus . . . then heard, cringing at the sound, the indrawn breath that crescendoed into a scream as I plunged past Howard Dolphs. One of his hands shot out to stay my flight, but I was past him and streaking into a room beyond.

It was a bedroom and there was only one small lamp burning, like the flicker of a votive candle beside a sarcophagus. Janet lay in the bed, on her side, her hair tumbled, her eyelids closed. Her face was as white as alabaster; long, dark lashes swept across the marble cheeks. One arm, the arm on which she was resting, dangled from the side of the bed: at the crook of the arm a slash gashed the white, velvety skin. From the gash blood oozed slowly, ran down the muscle of the forearm, forked into the limp, curved hand, trailed between the fingers, gathering in the pocket of the palm and then slowly, slowly, leisurely and thickly, seeped, drop by drop to the hardwood floor, forming a rich, crimson pool that, even as I watched, widened, spread, changed shape . . .

"Janet," I said, but it was only a whisper. Inaudible, really . . . but it didn't matter. She was way past hearing me . . . or anyone.

Chapter 20

I took a wavering step forward . . . and was seized from behind.

"Don't touch her."

I looked at Janet, quiet and dead, then opened my mouth to scream my protest. A hand clamped over my mouth. A hot breath steamed my face. "You," the man whispered, "you came here and ruined everything. I would have gotten her back. Somehow . . ."

A hand bruised my mouth; I tasted my own blood. "It's fantastic," Howard Dolphs said thinly. "Incredible that someone could . . . like the brick that falls on your head when you're out for a walk on a sunny day. That one person could do so much damage . . ."

With strength I hadn't known I was capable of, I wriggled free of his brute hand on my mouth. "Let me go," I screamed. "Get a doctor! Get a doctor! Please! Help her . . . please . . ."

"She's dead," he said, thickly. "What kind of fool *are* you? Can't you see she's dead? I was out, I came home and found her like this. And you . . . you're alive and well. While my darling lies dead. *Can't you see she's dead?* And that she came home . . . and I wasn't even here. Picture it," he said, his voice choking. "Just picture it. She had a drink . . . there's a glass in that other room. A bottle of vodka . . . and she ate some salted nuts. She waited . . . I wasn't here . . . and then she told herself it wasn't any use. She took my razor and cut her arms, bled to death . . ."

"You're sick, sick and crazy," I sobbed. "And Zoltan . . . both of you sick, crazy . . ."

"He's an old, desperate man. He's fighting for his life. And so was I. You stupid idiot. Between us, we had a living. But it was never that at all. The money . . . oh, no. Just Janet. It was a mystical thing. She loved me, never stopped loving me. Don't you even know what she was like? That she needed someone like me . . . always needed someone like me . . ."

The drip drip thundered into my eardrums. Let me die now, I thought. Let me not know another instant's horror, sadness, disillusion. Just let me die . . .

And then my moment of weakness evaporated. The children, Alex, the living . . . I made a heroic effort, and caught him off guard. Quickly, I was free of him. I dashed to the other room, heard his footsteps pounding behind me. I had my hand on the doorknob . . .

But he was on me, imprisoning me again. "What have I got to lose now?" he cried, exultantly. "Not with a whimper, but with a bang. I'll take you down with me. We'll go out together, both of us." His eyes, brilliant, stared into mine. "This is your last moment of life," he said, transported. "I'll watch you lose consciousness. It will give me great pleasure."

250

His hands went round my throat.

I struggled, gouging at his eyes, feeling his breath gust into my face, hearing his infuriated grunts. Somehow, I slipped out of his grasp and plunged forward, but it was no use. He grabbed me from behind and the iron fingers found my throat again, pressed brutally at the glands just below my chin. The pain was excrutiating and I cried out . . . but not for long.

Saliva welled into my mouth and I gagged; my eyes, filling with tears that felt like blood, were popping out of my head. I could feel the darkness closing in on me. My weapons were almost nil: the scratch of my nails down alien flesh that closed around my neck, a feeble stab of a heel at a target I couldn't even see.

I said, "Help me, someone . . . please . . ." I didn't know whether it was voiced or only in my mind. It was like drowning. Lights flashed, brilliant and multi-colored. Gagging, mumbling, I had a sudden sense of euphoria. Beautiful scenes flashed through my brain . . . the ineffable wonders of the unknown, of a life beyond this life, illumined the growing darkness. I fought, fought fiercely, but there was an insidious tug the other way, as I glimpsed the resplendent glory of the mysterious beyond, the ultimate release . . . and as the pressure increased on my throat I thought I saw a beautiful meadow where sheep grazed.

A green, peaceful meadow . . .

I wanted to put my hands to my neck. But my hands wouldn't move. I didn't even have any idea where my hands were. I couldn't feel them, couldn't feel anything except for the nausea and the gagging and the ghastly, shooting pain that sent arrows of agony from my throat to my head.

Try to remember, I said to myself. You have to remember . . .

Zoltan.

He was there suddenly, standing with his feet spread apart. That heavy body, like an elephant, clumsy, and—

Voices, staccato.

"What have you done to her?" Zoltan was saying.

"Killed her, of course. The way I killed that child of hers."

"What child?"

"She left the child on the beach. Naked. I killed it, tore it to pieces. She left her own child, just a baby."

Olympia.

"Take it easy, Howard. You didn't kill any child. You tried to kill this girl, in Chinatown. Didn't you?"

"I wish I had!"

"But you didn't. And she's not dead. Howard, we must talk this over. It's my fault, don't you understand? You must let me take care of everything. Just come quietly. We'll go some place and talk. But you don't want to kill anyone. It would mean that you'd have to go back. You don't want to go back, do you?"

"Go back?" A scream tore out of Howard and I thought of a seagull. The hoarse, harsh cry of a gull . . .

"Get away," he cried. "Get out, get out . . ."

"No." Zoltan took a step forward.

"Don't come near me!"

My eyes closed again. A terrible pain shot up, like a white-hot iron laid across my temples, and I groaned.

My eyes opened, as if a penknife has slitted them apart. Zoltan cursed and then he threw a heavy ring of keys into Howard's face.

I screamed. There was no sound. The scream was inside me. Howard Dolphs staggered, almost fell, as the keys struck him on the cheekbone. There was the soft tinkle of a clock striking.

Zoltan lunged.

I lay there, watching it.

I saw Howard reach behind the clock and then there was the blaze of metal. This time my scream sounded, arcing through the air, shrill and piercing. The haze cleared and I saw the revolver aimed. A shot rang out, and Zoltan's eyes opened wide. There was no sound from him. He simply staggered, stood wavering for a moment, and then slid down.

"Et tu, Brute," Howard said, and put his finger on the trigger again.

Once more my scream sounded, wild and animal, as I watched helplessly.

The first shot was wild; the man's hands were shaking so violently that he missed his own temple. The shot pinged through the pier glass; it shattered and fragmented. Little silver arrows of glass exploded.

But the second shot found its mark.

The sight was so horrifying that I turned away. I couldn't bear to see any more. I retched, and it was so excrutiatingly painful that the anguish of it brought tears to my eyes, and the agony shot through me, and the weakness took me down with it. The mists obscured everything, like the white, salt-drenched fogs of the city. There was an echo, reverberating in my mind, as I remembered the mirror breaking up when the bullet hit it. I thought of tear drops, thought of stained glass in a cathedral, shattering into brilliant, broken shards.

That was all. Velvet darkness was a pillow under my head.

Chapter 21

"Go away," I said.

"Katherine."

"Go away. Leave me alone, damn it."

"Katherine."

"Tell the nurse to come. I have a sore throat."

"Okay, she's coming around," the doctor said, and I realized that it must be the ether that was making me drowsy.

Or else I was blind.

"I can't open my eyes," I said gloomily. "Are the bandages still on?"

Had I paid my Blue Cross?

It would be just my luck to have let it lapse! When you were so damned busy all the time.

Suppose I had forgotten about it! It would be just my luck.

A man's voice sounded in my ear. *"I've always been unlucky . . . I suppose it's in the genes . . ."*

Everything fell away, the haziness, the plunging

darkness, the pleasant, comfortable feeling of release. Fright and horror suddenly seized me and I looked up and saw Alex bending over me. I heard a strange voice say, "Raise her head a little."

A scream was locked inside my throat. It was taking shape and form. It was building up, ready to explode.

"It's all right," Alex said quietly.

"Oh, Alex," I said. "Oh, let me die. Janet's dead and it's all my fault. Don't bring me back. Please God, oh please, let me be dead too."

His arms held me. Half-blinded, I saw the faces bending over me. Alex's face, and strangers' faces, men in blue uniforms. It was all like some ghastly tabloid cut . . . the screaming first page of a sensational newspaper. All those faces looking down at me . . .

It was not until later, much later, that what I had seen became real and true; that Zoltan had been dead when the others got there and that Howard Dolphs, cornered, had blown his brains out with a loaded revolver which had been, all the time, on the mantel above the old-fashioned fireplace.

But I never thought Janet, even if she had seen the revolver, would have used it. Men killed themselves with guns; women with sleeping caps . . . or a razor slash of the primary arteries. And ultimately I was grateful for one small thing: that Janet, unlike Howard, hadn't shot away half of her head but had died lovely and whole, with scarcely a scar on her perfect, youthful body.

It was a small thing to be grateful for, but at any rate was some minor compensation.

Chapter 22

It was Mrs. Lance who told me the whole story. Told Alex and me, and when she had finished I had learned a very hard lesson, namely to stop categorizing people, stop taking them at face value and instead give them credit for hidden values that didn't immediately show.

"What happened to Janet," she said, "was that she made a fatal, though not uncharacteristic mistake. She mistook pity and concern and compassion for love. What must have begun as a sexual dependency changed into something far more compelling, when she learned what Howard really was, that he was a hopeless schizophrenic. That he had been in a sanitarium for two years. That he was not answerable for his actions. That—"

She shook her head, with a kind of anger. "Why is it these people always find a savior of some kind? Janet . . . God, she fell into it just by luck. A girl like that whose compulsion was to *give*. I knew about Howard.

Her letters were full of him when she moved out here. It was the only time she ever turned to me at *all*. I knew something of what she was in for when she said she was in desperate trouble . . . that she had to talk about it . . ."

She pushed a strand of hair away from her forehead. "I didn't know what it was, just that there was something wrong about him, something . . . So you can imagine my delight when, after months and months went by, Janet wrote me that she had met a fine, wonderful man who had asked her to marry him. My elation was tempered with disappointment when there was no celebration. The announcement came to us after the ceremony."

"It was a quiet wedding at the Santa Maria mission," Alex said. "Janet wanted it that way."

"I had pictured champagne and myself in a beautiful dress," she said. "You know, I'm like that."

"We're all like that," I told her. "It's only natural."

"After all, she was an only child. At any rate, her letters stopped. It was as it had used to be. I wrote, but she didn't. For a whole long time, however, I was content. Janet was taken care of, and being musical myself, I was so happy to know that Alexander Saxon was my son-in-law."

She put out a hand and Alex took it. "I always will be proud of that," she said. "Well, then I read in the papers that you, Alex, were to conduct abroad, in London and Munich and then in Japan. I stopped writing because I thought you were both away. And then, to my surprise and shock, Janet showed up on our doorstep looking like a ghost. She hadn't gone with you. She unburdened herself, tearless, saying that she was just out of the hospital. She had given birth to a child and the father was—"

I saw the absolute incredulity in Alex's eyes. I would never tell him I knew. Never. His head reared back and his face was white. Mrs. Lance cleared her throat. She knew that what she was about to say would never, ever stop haunting her son-in-law.

"The father was Howard Dolphs."

It was Alex who broke the long silence.

"What happened to the baby?" he asked.

Mrs. Lance looked as if she had just eaten a very sour lemon. I've often noticed that when people are most affected they don't look tragic, or hollow-eyed, or bereaved. They simply look sick, nauseated. That was the way Janet's mother looked now.

"I'm going to finish this very quickly," she said. "Because it's all so upsetting." Her voice became breathless as she rushed on.

"When Janet first went to California, she settled in Santa Monica. And there, I later learned, made wonderful friends. Anne and Daniel Kaufman. Anne is an artist, like Jan, and Dan is a musicologist." She was looking intently at Alex. "It was through Dan Kaufman that you and Janet met. He knew you, not well, admittedly, but at least professionally. Oh, you weren't aware of the grand plan. But Dan felt he knew what he was doing. Perhaps he was wrong . . . at any rate, you were giving a concert in San Francisco. Janet went to that concert with the Kaufmans."

"Do you remember?" she asked.

"Yes, of course. Afterwards they came to the Green Room. That was my first meeting with Janet."

"And in a few months you and she were married.

259

I'm sure she was happy, Alex. I'm sure . . . if it hadn't been for Howard . . . but he must have been constantly on her mind, must, too, have been constantly after her. She could have *talked* to you, asked for your help, *asked* something of you. Instead, she bottled it all up inside her, and then . . . I don't know how many times . . . she went back to that house in Ghiradelli Square. And one fine day found herself pregnant."

There was a long, terrible silence. I sat examining my fingernails. Mrs. Lance simply waited, with a kind of practiced patience. Then Alex said, "I see. What you're telling me is that she was already pregnant when I went abroad for that European concert tour. And that's why she couldn't come with me."

Mrs. Lance nodded.

"Oh," he said. "So that was it."

Almost casually, he went on. "She was with him while I was away?"

"Yes. I think . . . I imagine she was considering going back to him for good."

"But she didn't," he said. "I wonder why?"

"No, you don't," she said. "You *know* what she really wanted, Alex. She wanted to shed that part of her life, but she couldn't. She wanted to live *your* life, the wonderful life you could give her, but she couldn't. There was too much of the old left over. There was too much Howard knew . . . or guessed. There was that child."

"She could have said it was our child," Alex said passionately.

"Janet? Oh, no. Not Janet. Everyone would have. *I*

would have. But not Janet. I think I can imagine what happened inside her at that point. She transferred everything to Howard. Her concern was for Howard. Her devotion. A sick, *sick* devotion. You were strong, successful, the hell with you."

She broke off and fluttered her pretty, manicured hands. "I can't seem to find my cigarettes," she said, and Alex got up and brought over a silver box. "Thank you," she said, blinking her eyes. She took a few, tremulous puffs and then looked up. "Well, at that, there isn't much more to tell. She went to a Catholic hospital, and there was much comforted by an order of nuns, The Little Sisters of the Poor. When the baby was born they assumed responsibility for the child, until such time as Janet was able to—"

The Little Sisters of the Poor, I was thinking. So that was why Janet had "occasionally" done volunteer work for them.

"And at last she turned to the Kaufman's again. They saw that she was in a serious decline, got her psychiatric help and wanted to take the baby, at least for a while. But Janet couldn't . . . couldn't say yes. She was playing for time, you see. She would, of course, be able to *make everything right*. Not just yet . . . but some day. She would tell you, find a way to make you understand."

"I would have understood," Alex said vehemently.

Mrs. Lance just looked at him, almost without expression. She didn't say anything. But we were both women, and I knew what she was thinking. She was thinking, no, you wouldn't have understood. You wouldn't, couldn't have forgiven.

261

So she just sat there and didn't comment.

"And then what happened, Mrs. Lance?" I asked. Somebody had to say something.

"Well, of course, the inevitable. Time went on, the way time has a way of going on, and Janet started doing good works for The Little Sisters of the Poor. Not very coincidentally, so did Anne Kaufman. And then, not surprisingly, the woman in the stronger position won. Anne lived in Sausalito, just across the bridge from San Francisco. Janet lived way out here in Big Sur. And soon had another baby, Alex Junior. The Kaufmans were, to their sorrow, unable to reproduce. And Janet, because she wasn't stupid, finally knew she had lost her child, a child who had formed a deep attachment to Anne Kaufman. After a while Anne pleaded with Janet to let her take the child, not for adoption, but simply to give a home to. It was too late, Janet finally realized. It was too late. She knew she could never . . . never . . . ."

There were sudden hot tears in Mrs. Lance's eyes. "And then the other children were born. Alex and Roger, the grandchildren I could see and touch and give presents to. Alex, this is the hardest thing of all," she said, trying to control her voice. "What I have to say now. A year ago Daniel Kaufman spoke to you about a musically talented little girl. He thought you might be interested in her gifts. You remember."

And now there was the longest silence of all. It was very quiet, so quiet that you could hear the groaning of the branches in the trees outside. The twitter of bird life seemed suddenly deafening. A clock ticked briskly.

"Fleur?" Alex said at last, and I scarcely recognized his voice. It sounded . . . rusty, somehow.

"Yes, Alex."

"Fleur?" He got up and looked down at Mrs. Lance. *"Fleur?"*

"She's part of Janet," Mrs. Lance said, sobbing.

I saw that tall man, Alexander Saxon, look down with wonder, and then with disbelief; with utter stupefaction he walked off a few paces, stood looking out the window, then abruptly left the room.

Mrs. Lance sat there, her shoulders heaving. I got up and went to her. "All right," I said. "Cry it out, Caroline. I'm so sorry. For everything. For us all. For Janet."

For Janet.

Mrs. Lance held a tissue to her trembling lips. "It's been so difficult," she said, choked. "Outlining the sad progress of Janet's life this way. It's been so terrible. Like exposing her, all her sad dreams, her tragic dilemmas . . ."

She leaned against me and wept. "Why should she have come to such an end?" She bowed her head. "She stopped hating me, you know. She was glad to have me here. That's the only thing I—that's what I'll have to remember, that she wanted her mother near her. I don't know why and I don't think she knew why, but it helped her, somehow. To have me here."

"I'm sure it did. I know it did. Mrs. Lance, who was Zoltan?"

"Why, he was a male nurse in the sanitorium where Howard spent some time," she said. "He was very good with Howard, and Janet was grateful." Her face

263

grew bitter and bright. "In fact, so grateful that she would have provided for Zoltan for the rest of his life. He didn't have to . . . to . . . to do what he did. He didn't have to!"

"He was a weak man," I said. "In fact a frightful man. Howard was sick. But Zoltan . . .

I felt unutterably weary.

"He was the real culprit in Janet's life," I finally said. "His was the greatest guilt."

But in my heart I knew it wasn't true. Alex was the real culprit, and I was. Yes, I thought, almost drained of emotion. If there was a villain in the piece, it was I. Who had, even if it was at Alex's behest, interrupted the natural flow of things. There were many ways of living, and perhaps Janet's way had been right for her. A terrible way . . . but a way she had chosen.

Mine, I felt, was the ultimate culpability. I, who had loved Janet, had been the instrument of her destruction. And I knew I would live with that knowledge for the rest of my days. Forever, until I died.

And then Alex came back.

He looked haggard and his eyes were bleak. But he knelt at Janet's mother's feet. "You're a wonderful woman," he said. "I've always felt that. I always will. And your daughter, my wife, was a lovely, dear—"

His voice faltered. "It's just that now I can never make up to her for—"

"None of us can," Mrs. Lance said. "She was a brave, troubled woman. She had her faults, God knows, but all the same she was a very unusual, tender personality and I'm proud to have brought her into the world. She was a misfit, in a way, but then I've always been partial to the ones who didn't quite fit into the rigid scheme of things. I'm only very ordinary, and so is Ed, but between us we made that lovely girl . . . our Janet."

She broke down completely then, and hid her face in her hands.

Alex went to her. "If only I could, in some way, have made it easier for Janet. And for you."

"You can now," she said, raising her head. "And it will be rugged, Alex. Fleur must be told, and that's your job. It's your place to let her know the truth, and watch over her. She's in your hands now, forever."

Chapter 23

In the early part of my visit to California, the whole group of us had gone to the redwood forests. It was a picnic outing; the children had been asking for just such a treat. The day was beautiful, with the vast, unbroken sky as blue as the purest sapphire and the cloud formations so breathtaking that your heart broke with the sheer beauty of them.

Gertrude and Tony and Fleur and I had made a lunch. Hard-boiled eggs and small tomatoes, oily Greek olives and succulent, pimento-filled green ones, potato and macaroni salad, and maybe a million sandwiches. We had a fine time, under the towering trees. It was cool enough for sweaters. The children were such fun, listening to Zoltan tell about the meaning of the circles on the trunks of the gigantic trees.

"This," he had said, "is a century, this little ring here." He pointed to the next ring. "Here's another, and another, and another."

"How many centuries?" Roger asked excitedly.

Zoltan looked up. Some of the sequoias, almost four hundred feet in height, seemed to pierce the sky above. "Oh . . . maybe 300 . . . maybe 400 . . ."

"Gee . . . gee . . ."

We had our picnic and then, gathering up the paper bags, walked on, and on, and on. And I remember that I had a strange reaction. The trees, some of them thousands of years old, dwarfed us. I felt humbled as I had never been humbled in my life. We were so little, so ineffectual; pigmies, in fact. The contrast between our own abbreviated lives and those of nature's gods, the long-lived, giant monoliths that watched the centuries go by, was almost shattering.

I listened to the laughter and chatter of Janet's two little boys and thought: they'll be men soon, and then old men, and then they'll die. And it was only a moment in time.

Alex happened to be walking beside me, and I suppose he noticed my silence, my sudden melancholy. "Are you despondent?" he asked. "Many persons crumble, psychically, in these surroundings. There have been random cases of suicide here. I can understand that. It's a little terrifying. You feel like a grain of sand, only an atom in the grand design. Which, of course, is what we are."

I let him talk. My own throat was too tight for speech.

"A speck in the universe," he went on. "All our sufferings gone unnoticed."

My hand was suddenly in his.

"This is the forest primeval," he said softly, and his fingers tightened over mine. "Don't be sad, though.

We *are* important. Our destinies, insignificant as they may seem to be at this moment, *do* mean something. It was so decreed, from the moment man left the green slime. Tiny as we are, we vanquish what we must, conquer enormous odds. Men have souls, Katherine, and will die for a beautiful dream."

Some day I may see the redwood trees again. When enough time has passed. But not yet, not yet.

I keep up a regular correspondence with Alexander Saxon. And with his wife too; Miriam Saxon, formerly Miriam Sellaby. Dennis' mother. There is quite a large household out there, at Xanadu. Husband and wife and children. Dennis, Fleur, Alex Junior and Roger. And a baby, a little girl named Janet.

I still live in Manhattan, that troubled borough of New York, but I no longer do crass, commercial work. I don't need to. Because one evening, at a cocktail party, I met a very pleasant man, an artist like myself, and these days don't have to worry about where the next dollar is coming from.

But that's not what it's *about*.

What it's about is that I found what I wanted, what I had hoped for, what makes my life meaningful and rich and wonderful. In short: I fell in love again. Only this time it was something I could handle, something I didn't have to feel guilt about. And I'm very much in love. Imagine it: I married a Hungarian. The second Hungarian to come into my life. I think the main reason he was drawn to me was that, when I met him and there were other attractive young women in the room, I had a trump card to play. Thanks to Janet. I don't know why I thought of it, or how I remembered it after all that time . . . but I did.

He said to me, "You're very pretty, Kip."

And I answered, "*Koszonom Szepen*."

How could I *possibly* have remembered that?

"It means 'thank you'," Janet had said, on the sundeck at Xanadu.

He asked me, after laughing uproariously, what I was doing for dinner that evening.

And it went on from there.

We live on Sutton Place. Because it's quiet and country-like, and there aren't many sections like that left in Manhattan. Our living room is thirty by forty, though most of the other rooms are little more than cubicles. But in that large, spacious living room, on the north wall, a portrait dominates the room.

The painting Janet did of me, in the Fortuny dress.

The first time Norma visited us, she stood at the door leading into the living room and said, "Oh, Kip, what a lovely portrait of Janet."

And it does look like Janet.

It should, because some of me *is* Janet.

We are shaped by others, by the lives that surround and girdle us. And so, in some strange, wonderful way, even though Janet is dead, she lives on, through me as well as through her own children.

She lives.

What we have known and loved gilds the future. The present, metaphysically speaking, doesn't really exist; what is now becomes, even at the moment of recognition, already the past. And so we live, with shining anticipation, for what *will* be. What *has* been clings to us tenaciously, claims us in a thousand ways, is never completely shed; the future is the wondrous landscape of expectation and hope. What tomorrow offers is the great promise that makes our lives meaningful. And what has been and is now over is, irreconcilably and forever, beyond recall.

LOOK FOR OUR MAGNUM CLASSICS